COSMIC JUNKMAN

By
ROG PHILLIPS

ARMCHAIR FICTION
PO Box 4369, Medford, Oregon   97501-0168

*For more information about Armchair Books and products, visit our
website at…*

www.armchairfiction.com

Or email us at…

armchairfiction@yahoo.com

DO ROBOTS DREAM OF PLAYING FETCH?

Earth's military forces had a unique way of fielding an army. They took the brains of dogs, wiped their memories, and trained them with just the right amount of discipline. Then, they were placed in the bodies of robots that were then used to fight Earth's battles in outer space. What would happen, though, if those dog brains started to regain their memories? What kind of carnage might be released upon humanity if an army of vengeance-seeking robots were loosed upon the Earth? To make matters worse, an alien visitor had exactly that idea—and he had two million robot bodies to help make his invasion plans into reality!

Veteran sci-fi author Rog Phillips spins a taut tale of futuristic espionage, intrigue, and betrayal in this fine novel of an alien invasion.

FOR A COMPLETE SECOND NOVEL, TURN TO PAGE 89

CAST OF CHARACTERS

LARRY JACKSON
He was assigned to track down a runaway robot—he just hadn't counted on falling for Stella, who didn't want him to succeed!

STELLA GAMBLE
She was afraid of the robots, but she was more afraid of going broke. So, she came up with a plan—and it wasn't very nice!

2615 (aka ROVER)
This robot had no inhibitions about killing humans and had a very good reason to kill them—revenge against humanity!

PWOWP
Gathering up a few new brains was no problem, what he really needed was an army of brainless robots to put them in!

VILBIS
This dictatorial mastermind of the opposing forces in the last war believed he was still indispensible.

THE JUNKMAN
His job was to gather all the robots after a war, then place the good ones in storage and scrap the rest.

CHAPTER ONE

Log Report:
Fleet: Alpha Aquilae; 20,080 surviving ships.
Flagship ROVER.
Personnel: human;
Fleet Admiral William A. Ford
Vice Admiral Paul G. Belcross
robot;
2,649,366 (Ids. appended)
passenger: (human);
Generalissimo Vilbis (prisoner under w.c.a.)
Dates May 7, 4765;
flight formation arrow, speed 1,700,000 m.p.s.
Scheduled date of arrival at Earth: June II, 4766
Distance from Earth on Earth-Aquilae axis: ten light years.

"RUMMY," Vilbis said, reaching through the hand-hole in the inch thick laminated glass wall of his prison and spreading his cards on the table. His lips formed into the cruel haughty smile that had been his trademark to billions of humans for almost half a century. His wide-set black eyes mocked the other two players.

"Well, well," Paul Belcross smirked. "I see now why you lost the war, Vilbis. Isn't that a six of diamonds in your heart sequence?"

The black eyes glanced down. The long-fingered hand began to retrieve the cards, then paused. Vilbis' almost classic features darkened with anger. With an effort he became calm. A secret inner amusement made little lights in his eyes as he looked up at his two captors again.

"You know," Bill Ford said thoughtfully, "sometimes I think you must have some kind of an ace up your sleeve. You don't seem at all concerned that this is your last trip. The War Crimes Court—then death by hanging." Bill frowned. "Could be you figured the angle I've always worried about. The Federation is always too quick to demobilize the robots after a war. Some day some punk like you is going to take that into consideration. He's going to surrender, but have a reserve space navy waiting until Earth is without defenses, then take over and win."

"Too bad I didn't think of that when I could have done something about it," Vilbis said too cheerfully.

"Maybe you did think of it," Bill said. "When we get home I'm going to suggest we keep the Aquilae Fleet mobilized for at least ten years."

"You know they won't do that," Paul Belcross said. "They're more afraid of the robots than they are of attack. So am I, actually."

"We're just afraid of what they could do if they got free," Bill said. "Their potential intelligence is greater than human. If they overcame their built-in instinct for obedience to human command they could—why think of what our two million robots could do!"

"Why all this discussion of robots?" Vilbis asked. "They're just dogs. Not even that. They were dogs for six months of their existence before their brains were transplanted into synthegell fluid by the mind transplant machine." His eyes took on a far away look. His voice became regretful. "I had a hundred thousand scientists working on that problem. If the mind of one dog could be transplanted into synthegell without destroying the dog's brain there would be no limit to the production of robot brain cartridges. If we could have licked that problem I'd have won the war."

"If!" Paul spat. "You're a renegade Earthman. I'm putting in my application to be the one to hang you as soon as we get home."

"How do you—" Vilbis clamped his lips closed and scooped up his cards.

"How do we know we'll get home?" Bill Ford said. "Is that what you were going to say?"

Vilbis looked at his cards casually. "No," he said absently. "I was going to say how do you expect to play cards and talk at the same time?"

A raucous blast exploded in the room. Bill and Paul stared at each other in surprise. Vilbis smiled.

Bill leaped across the room to the cm board. He jabbed at buttons. A giant screen lit up, showing a spaceship. Smaller screens lit up, revealing robot ship commanders.

"Look at that ship, Paul," Bill said. "You know them all. Aquilanean, Centaurian, Cygnian. It isn't any known type—and with a war just over, there hasn't been time to mass-produce new types." He jabbed at a button. "All ships," he said. "All ships. Defense formation five. Five. Operation three. Three." He listened to the repeats.

PAUL Belcross had leaped to the huge tri-di sphere and turned it on. Seconds later both men, Vilbis forgotten but watching with bright eyes, were studying the small dots in the tri-di. The flight formation in the shape of a giant arrow was quickly changing shape as the fleet formed a defensive sphere around the flagship and its human occupants. The *Rover* was the only bright blue dot. The others were red.

But now other dots were materializing at the outer

fringe of the tri-di, too many new dots to count. Approaching ships.

Across the room a voice from a loudspeaker was saying, "Eighty seconds to contact. No response. No response."

"Another second and they'll be within range," Paul said.

"God!" Bill's voice exploded. His eyes were on the large area of the tri-di where ships had abruptly ceased to exist.

"Something's wrong with the tri-di," Paul said. "No weapon could do that."

"Nothing's wrong with the tri-di," Bill said sharply. "And we don't have that kind of weapon. They're something alien. Have to be. Some other galaxy. There's always been that possibility."

A rapidly repeated pip-pip-pip came from the cm board. Bill leaped to it. A light, under a small screen showing a robot, was blinking. He pressed the button. The robot saluted. His Id was stamped across his chrome chest, with four gold stars after it. "We will be destroyed, sir," it said. "Would suggest Flagship *Rover* change course forty degrees at eight o'clock and go on without fleet."

"You're giving orders?" Bill said, his face going pale and his eyes narrowing—not at the impending defeat, but at this sign of independent initiative in a robot.

"It's your only chance for survival," the robot said. "It must be done at once."

"Place yourself under ship arrest and give me the next in command," Bill ordered sharply. The screen went blank. "That's mutiny!" he shouted, unbelieving.

Vilbis, behind his glass wall, laughed aloud.

"Not mutiny," Paul said. "They are gone. All our ships are gone!" His voice conveyed the incredulous horror in his mind.

In the tri-di there was only the bright blue dot, and the thousands of approaching ships of the enemy.

The next instant the ship lurched violently.

"They're boarding!" Bill shouted. "But they aren't going to get Vilbis back alive."

He leaped to a locker and opened it with clumsy fingers, bringing out a g.i. raygun. He turned to leap toward the glass wall separating him from Vilbis. Before he could take a step a large section of a bulkhead vanished in smoke. For a brief instant Bill and Paul stared with unbelieving eyes at what entered the room.

Then they died.

"Stop!" The word exploded from Vilbis's lips. He stared at the cooked flesh that had been his captors. Then his eyes lifted to the jagged hole in the bulkhead.

"You fools!" he spat. His lips curled with cold anger. "Where do you hope to get two other humans now?"

CHAPTER TWO

THE demobilization station trailed the Earth, a million and a half miles behind and in the same orbit around the Sun. It was shaped like a thick disc. At the moment there were five ships resting against one surface of the station. Three of them were warships. One was a Federation ship. The fifth was a giant freighter with SURPLUS JUNK CO. painted on it in bold blue letters.

Each of the five ships was attached to the space station underneath its hulk by short airlocks containing elevators. These led down into the station where air pressure was kept at fifteen pounds.

Inside the station, robots were emerging from the elevators leading to the three warships. The robots were all identical except for their ID numbers across their metallic chests. Arms and legs of metal rods and joints in almost exact duplication of human bones, torso shaped like a metal box, short neck joint supporting a head that was little more than two four inch glass lenses, two rod-microphones, and a small voice box.

The emerging robots moved at orders snapped by a human and marched toward a building fifty yards away, where they lined up at attention and became motionless.

Two humans moved swiftly down the line, behind the lined up robots. At each robot one of them twisted a copper colored disk in the robot's back, carefully drew out a cylinder eight inches long and four inches in diameter, and handed the cylinder to the other, who lowered it into a plastic case. These cylinders were the brains of the robots. They were destined for the Federal ship—and storage until the next war.

While the robot brain was being lowered into its plastic storage case by the one man, the first lifted the now demobilized robot body and placed it on a cart, already stacked high with similar bodies. The immediate destination of these bodies was the junk company freighter.

If the robots were aware of what was about to happen to them as they waited, they gave no indication, no protest. Their lens eyes were directed straight ahead of them, unmoving—except for one robot.

The ID across its chest was 532-03-2615 followed by four gold stars. Its head was turned just enough so that it could see down the line. Its rod microphones were turned so that it could listen…

"That junkman gives me the creeps, Joe," the man placing brain cylinders into plastic cases grumbled.

"That's because he's a creep, Mel. Here. Take this."

He thrust a brain cylinder at his companion.

"Hey! Careful!" Joe said, almost dropping it.

Mel chuckled and flipped the robot body, almost weightless on the station here in space, carelessly to the top of the stack on the truck.

"Here comes junky now, Joe," he said.

"Don't damage the bodies. Don't damage the bodies." The figure that approached, pushing an empty truck, wore a dirty and well worn civilian suit that seemed even more decrepit in contrast to the neat military uniforms. His skin was leathery. A pair of glasses hung on his hawkish nose, their thick lenses magnifying the close-set eyes underneath, and making them seem to lie on the inner surfaces. His lips were partly open, but never seemed to move while he talked. "There was a cracked lens on one," he accused.

"What's the matter, junky?" Joe grinned. "If we get a scratch on one it's still two hundred pounds of scrap metal—or were you planning on using the bodies?" He and Mel laughed.

"Who knows?" the junkman said. "I only follow my orders. No scratches. No damage to the bodies. Who knows? Maybe they go into storage until the next war." He reached with a dirty hand to clutch at Mel's lapel, but didn't make it. "I'll show you," he said. "*Two* of them are damaged. Not worth seventeen credits."

"Can't stop now," Mel said. "We want to get done by quitting time. Joe has a date."

"Come on," the junkman said. "You've got to look. I have to have witnesses when I hand in my report on the carelessness of the military."

"Oh, all right," Mel said. He and Joe followed the dusty junkman around the building.

The instant they were out of sight, 2615 moved, running

swiftly around the other end of the building. It reached a vantage point where its lens eyes could watch the three figures when they emerged from the elevator to the ship above.

It watched Joe and Mel return to their work. It waited until the junkman had gone for another truckload of demobilized robot bodies. Then, swiftly, it ran to the elevator. At the top it sent the elevator back down, then faced the tiers of frames that filled the vast hold of the ship. Most of them now held inert robot shapes.

2615 chose an empty rack and climbed in, lying face up. It looked no different than any of the thousands of other forms.

It remained motionless. The junkman returned with load after load. Eventually the hold was filled. Clanging and whirring noises told of preparations for departure.

Acceleration pushed the robot deeper into the protective foam rubber of its rack. It waited…

FEAR. It began in the eyes of the cataloguer when his sorting machine came to a stop on the ID card for 532-03-2615. It grew as a terrible, animating force that drained blood from faces and made hands clumsy, as the checking and rechecking on 2615 began. It spread through networks of communication wires. It stopped at the borders of news release, lest it spread over the world.

Fear organized itself, finally, settling into a pasty expression, unnatural eyes, and drumming fingers. The expression and eyes and fingers belonged to Carl Wilson, chief of the Demobilization staff. It centered there, but its aura spread out over the backwash it had left. Fear lurked in the hushed silence. Fear rode as an undertone in the slightest sound, lay ready to spring from behind every door.

Larry Jackson felt it as he gave the receptionist his name.

Stella Gamble was oblivious of it as she pushed into the waiting room.

Larry looked at her and wished it was his day off and a girl like her was with him. He wondered what her name was.

"I'm Stella Gamble," Stella said to the receptionist. "I've got to see Mr. Wilson at once. My freighter is overdue with two million junked robots. Something's got—"

"Will you please be seated, Miss Gamble?" the receptionist said firmly. Then, "You may go right in, Mr. Jackson. Mr. Wilson is waiting for you."

It was then Stella and Larry looked into each other's eyes. Hers were narrowed, sizing him up, guessing what he was and why he was there. His were friendly, smiling.

"Thanks," he murmured to the receptionist. He went toward the door, conscious of Stella's eyes following him. He went in.

"*There* you are, Jackson," Wilson said, running fingers through his iron gray hair in nervous relief. "You've guessed why—"

"Yes," Larry said.

Behind him the door opened violently. Sharp heels clicked on the floor. "Mr. Wilson," Stella demanded. "I know why this man is here. You're going to give him instructions to blast my freighter out of existence the minute he can—"

"You're Stella Gamble?" Wilson said. "I've heard of you. Will you please wait in the reception room until I finish with—"

"Larry Jackson," Stella pronounced the name. Her wide set blue eyes showed scorn. "The man who is going to kill one of my men and destroy my ship and its cargo just to get at a robot."

"*Just* to get at a robot?" Wilson said indignantly. "You must be out of your head!" He picked up an oblong of paper on his desk and thrust it at Larry. "The junkship has been traced three hundred million miles out by routine radar. You can pick it up from there by ion tracking—we hope. Don't take any chances. *Destroy that ship!*" His lips trembled. "Even if the pilot is still on it. It's one life against..." He didn't complete the thought.

"Against fear," Stella said. "You are all cowards. Afraid of a dog because it could turn against you."

"Afraid of an *intelligence*," Wilson said wearily. His lips pulled back in a weak grin. "So are you. You're just more afraid of going broke."

Larry folded the paper and put it in his pocket. He turned toward the door. Stella clutched his sleeve, stopping him. She spoke swiftly, pleading. "Let me go with you. I'm capable. Give me a chance to go down and reason with that robot. If it doesn't work..."

Larry looked at her upturned face, the lips that could smile or laugh more naturally than pout, the wide-set eyes that could do things to him at any other time. He thought, it's a shame I won't ever get the chance. "Sorry, Miss Gamble," he said stiffly, "I'm on duty, and I'm not permitted to take passengers with me."

He went on toward the door, feeling his sleeve tear at her nails as she tried to hold him longer.

"It's very unfortunate—" Wilson said as Larry opened the door.

"If I can't go with him after my freighter I'm going after

it on my own!" Stella said as he closed the door.

Larry put his fingers to his lips for the benefit of the receptionist and swiftly side-stepped to a filing cabinet where he stooped down out of sight.

The next instant the door from Wilson's office burst open again, hanging against the wall. Stella's eyes searched the office. She ran to the hall door, and out.

Larry bounded back into Wilson's office. Wilson said, "Whew!" and mopped his brow, then pointed to his private entrance. Larry nodded and left.

CHAPTER THREE

IT was a world of hard whites and bottomless blacks, with the hard whites so close they gave you the feeling you could reach out and touch them. Then you blinked your eyes and they were holes in infinity through which loneliness poured. That was space. Sure, there was the Earth somewhere aft of the rockets' red glare, and the Moon, looking like high-priced models against a velvet backdrop.

But you didn't look at them, because the stars were points on a tri-di screen, and you were back in school working a problem in navigation and hoping you didn't get a wrong answer.

You loved it—or you went crazy. Larry loved it. Or maybe it wasn't love. It was like a woman. It was in his blood.

He stopped punching the keys of the calculator and used both hands to press the studs controlling the gyro motors, watching the needles of gyro meters until they pointed to the right numbers.

He took several deep breaths, squirming back in his seat against the form-fitting cushion of foam rubber. He made sure his elbows rested securely in their little niches so that his arms wouldn't pull out of their sockets.

Then he touched the controls, feeling the surge of power as his ship, an SP47, responded, hearing the subsonic vibration around him as atoms broke into little bits in the fission chambers of the rockets and spewed out of them into space.

The G needle moved past three, past four, past five. It moved into the part of the dial where the glossy white changed to pink. It crept slowly toward the darker pink, toward the deep red.

I don't WANT an ice cream cone. It was his sister's voice, real as audible sound. He had been six years old when she had said that, back in Springfield.

The voices came. The images came. Vivid and unimaginative. True reproductions. That's what acceleration did to the brain. It squeezed the juke out of brain cells into nerve networks. It could get you—

Larry jerked back to an awareness of what he was doing. Sweating, he coaxed the G needle back down a little. Not much.

It had been close. Why had he done it? Fear. He could let himself realize that, now that he was alone. Fear of a robot that had stolen a ship and gone out into space, when robots only obeyed orders. It was an instinctive thing, bred in all men for generations.

You ought to be whipped! That was dad. Good old dad. Larry had been about nine then. He had run away— hitchhiked four hundred miles to watch a spaceship leave the ground and climb up out of sight.

Pip-pip, pip-pip, pip-pip.

Larry lifted his fingers from the controls gradually in response to the signal from the board. The G needle dropped back into the white.

The voices were gone, the images, the thoughts. He grinned on one side of his face. This was the end of the radar line. Now his work would begin. Around his ship charged ions were streaming past. Some of them would have come from the junk ship.

The *tracker*, a sensitive electronic instrument projecting from the shell, would read them—their concentration, velocity, and direction. From that he could project the position and, trajectory of the junk ship.

Or maybe he could see it already.

He flicked on the video eyes of the ship and waited for the screen to light up. There *was* a ship ahead.

The fear bit into him like acid. As quickly, it vanished. The stern outline of the ship ahead was not that of a freighter. It was a small job. Private, in the LR class— probably an LR65.

AN absurd thought flashed into his mind. It couldn't be. Stella Gamble could have put a line on him, but she would have had to wait until he went into full acceleration before she could have calculated his direction.

But she would have blacked out trying to follow him. No girl and few men could have kept up with him. None could have gotten ahead of him into that position.

He turned on the radio and set it at commercial communication. He waited impatiently until the warm-up tube went off.

"Look astern and identify yourself," he said sharply.

"Hello, Larry," a triumphantly impudent and very familiar voice purred from the loudspeaker. "My ship is the LR65, *Hell Bat*."

"Miss Gamble—Stella!" Larry sputtered. "What are you

doing—"

"Never mind that now, spaceman," her voice came, businesslike. "I've got his track coming in. Keep out of my way. That's all I ask. Give me time to do it my way. You can always destroy the freighter later—if I don't succeed.

"Sure," Larry said bitterly. "I can always destroy a ship that has a girl in it I could like—" He bit his lip.

Her laugh answered him. She was drawing away from him.

Muttering a curse, he extended his *trackers* from the shell, but even as he did, he realized the trick she had played on him. Her own exhaust trail would make it impossible for him to detect that other fainter trail.

And there was something else.

"Miss Gamble!" he spoke into the microphone sharply. "Stella! That robot could leave a space mine. Your ship is a private job. It doesn't have the equipment in it to get away from a mine."

Her laugh was unbelieving, scornful. "And where could that robot get a space mine?" she taunted.

"It could make one. It has the materials."

CHAPTER FOUR

2615 endured the acceleration with impatience. It would lift an arm and hold it still, feeling how much effort it took. All the time it kept its gleaming eyes of polished glass fixed intently on the hatch to the pilot compartment.

Finally it slid out of the rack and climbed upward toward that closed hatch, sure that it would not open under such induced weight. It took a long time to climb the distance.

When 2615 reached the closed hatch, it looked around

for a place to hide and wait. There was none. All interior structure had been stripped away to make room for racks for the robot bodies.

The robot examined the hatch closely. It became motionless, as though thinking things out. Abruptly, it twisted the wheel that pulled in the locking rods. Nothing now held the cover closed except the tremendous acceleration of the ship.

It directed its gaze downward at its feet, searching for more solid support. With slow deliberation it set itself, then placed its metal hands against the cover.

For several seconds nothing happened. Then the cover lifted slightly on one side, pivoting on its hinges. Inch by slow inch it went up, until it balanced on edge.

The robot took one hand away tentatively. With slow caution it forced its weight against the acceleration, up into the opening. One slip, one misstep, and the hatch cover would have slammed down on its upturned eyes and ears and voice box, smashing them beyond repair.

Its feet went up through. It looked around, and found itself in a circular well. But here were places to hide. Open hatchways leading off the well.

It straddled the open hatchway and slowly lowered the cover until it was in place again. It twisted the wheel that shot the rods into their sockets, locking the hatch.

As it began to straighten up, the acceleration ended. Gears and pistons tensed against tremendous weight now moved with the force of a violent leap. Instantaneous reflexes adapted to the change. The robot caught at an open hatch hole halfway up the well.

The space inside was small and empty. The robot climbed in. A few seconds later metallic sounds exploded sharply from outside. It looked up and saw the hatch at the top of the well open, the junkman appear, looking down and then climbing through the hole into the well.

The robot withdrew its head and waited.

The junkman was humming an indistinguishable tune. The sound approached. The robot braced itself, one hand ready to reach out.

The unmusical humming stopped, then took up again, growing remote. Quickly the robot looked out. The well was empty. The junkman had gone through one of the hatch openings farther up.

The humming stopped. The junkman's voice spoke. "Well, well, my friend. We have come to the end of the road, for you. I kept you alive in case something happened. Now I can dispense with you."

There was a deep groan. A different voice said thickly, "Damn you, go ahead and kill me."

"That I will do. You should thank me for it. Broken ribs from the acceleration. I will kill you. Yes. But I can't have your body floating in space where it might be picked up. No one must know that you didn't steal this ship yourself. You get tied to a space mine... So. Now I kill you—So!"

2615 moved from the hatch opening and up the well to where the voices emerged. It paused briefly while its glittering eyes took in the scene.

THE dusty junkman was just straightening up from the inert form lashed cruelly around the black sphere of a g.i. space mine. His back was toward the opening.

Careful, so as not to make a sound, the robot slid through the opening and gathered itself for a leap. At that instant, the junkman seemed to sense its presence. He whirled around just as the robot leaped.

2615 saw its fist enter the junkman's face, sinking inches deep.

Then, impossibly, it saw the human seize its metal arm and twist it as if it were putty. The human face was gone. The human head dangled at a broken angle.

Tangled thoughts within the robot brain meshed into desperate action. It was futile. Its other arm was twisted. Its legs were wrapped into grotesque spirals.

Garbled sound came from the smashed human face. The junkman went away.

2615, helpless to move, studied the body tied to the space mine. A gaping hole in the chest was still spurting blood. A shudder shook the dying man, then he was still.

Nothing moved for a long time. Then there was movement outside the hatch opening. An arm dressed in the sleeve of a space officer poked in. It was followed by a face bearing the stamp of authority. The space officer straightened up and looked down at the robot.

"So," he said. "A robot. I hadn't expected that. You almost got me. If you had hit me in the chest instead of the head it would be all over. Lucky I have plenty of bodies of every description. Human bodies. Your kind wouldn't fit me."

"You—a robot?" 2615 said.

The space officer stared at the robot, frowning. "And what if I am?" he said.

"If I had known that I wouldn't have attacked you. I— I wanted to add you to—that." The robot turned its head toward the space mine. It added, "I thought you were *human*."

"Mm hmm," the space officer said, nodding. "I can understand that. You hate humans."

"Yes."

"How would you like to help me destroy them? All of them!"

A twisted metal arm twitched. "Put my brain in another body," the robot said.

"That I will do," the space officer said. "But let me warn you these bodies of mine are made of better stuff than yours. One bit of treachery and I'll cripple you again."

Fifteen minutes later the space officer returned with a robot body. Callously he turned the helpless robot over. He twisted the copper-colored disc and drew out the brain cylinder. As carefully, he inserted it in the hollow receptacle of the undamaged body. He stepped back and watched curiously.

2615 lay motionless for several seconds. Abruptly one of its arms moved. It turned over and sat up, then rose carefully to its feet.

"Very nice," the space officer said. "Now put the mine in the airlock and we'll leave it for anyone who might be following us."

2615 obeyed. Then it turned slowly to the space officer. There was admiration in its tones. "You have the perfect answer," it said. "With human-like bodies you can go anywhere. But—I thought I was the first robot to ever escape."

"So, far as I know, you are," the spaceman said. "You see, I'm—but I think I will have to make sure of you before I say more."

CHAPTER FIVE

THE space mine was round and dead black. Unreflecting. It drifted out a little as the long length of the

junk freighter moved ahead, and blended into the blackness of space. The dead man, twisted around it at a
grotesque angle, would have appeared to be someone
almost doubled over backwards with mirth, if there had
been any eyes to see him.

When the freighter had gone, pulling ahead at one G
acceleration, the mine began to spin slowly, making the
dead man seem to be searching for something—or seeing
some far-off horror that caused his eyes to bulge out.

After a while there was a solid click from the interior of
the space mine. A soft whine rose upward toward a
supersonic pitch. Small holes appeared in the black surface
of the globe, and small shapes crept out. Some of them
were under the man, pushing at him. But the ropes held.

The mine didn't spin any more. The dead man seemed
to have already forgotten the freighter, looking back the
way it had come, waiting for what was to come next.

Imperceptibly it froze over with a microfilm, of
crystalline ice, so that new stars seemed to spring into
being.

And that's the way Stella saw it. She hadn't taken Larry
seriously about the space mine, and was only trying to
catch her first glimpse of her freighter.

It didn't seem real. It was a face that looked somehow
familiar, with two thick white spikes protruding from its
nostrils like mockeries of tusks.

A thought flashed through her mind that Larry Jackson
had figured out some dirty trick to scare her with. She
didn't have much time to think before she knew that what
she was seeing was real. Its position was such that it
should have passed ten miles to the side.

It started to. The marble monster with tusks didn't turn
to follow her. Then three things happened. Stella

recognized the man. He was the pilot she had assigned to the junk ship. Stella saw the sphere he was tied to.

And fire shot out from that circular void. Her pilot swung toward her again and rushed at her like the figurehead on the prow of an ancient watership.

"Larry!" Stella screamed into the radio.

"I see it," his voice answered her. "Get on your spacesuit and jump out. Turn on your suit radio so I can find you afterwards. Every second counts!"

In the airlock with the shell door open, she looked into bottomless space and drew back. Then she closed her eyes and leaped. When she opened them again there were no stars, only bright white lines that all went in the same direction, and for an instant a bright yellow splotch that was like a gold band circling her far out.

She knew what the white lines were. She pressed the right button on her chest, and pressure seized her shoulders gently. It was the suit gyro, and after a while it slowed the lines until they became stars.

She remembered then to turn on her radio, feeling panic grip her at the thought that maybe Larry wouldn't find her. The fire from his rockets was small, far away. That's all she could see other than the stars. And her stomach was telling her there was no gravity to hold it in position.

Then she heard Larry in her suit radio. "I've got you beamed, Stella. I'll follow down slowly. Are you all right?"

"Yes," she said, anger and frustration in her voice.

"I can see you now," Larry said.

IT was another hour before he had maneuvered so he could let her drift toward the open spacelock of the SP47 and she could feel her gloved hands touch something solid.

Then she was standing up. Larry was taking her helmet

off and she was unzipping her suit. He was trying to look stern and reprimanding and she was trying to look defiant and unafraid.

"Don't think this earns you anything," she snapped.

"I hope the *Hell Bat* represented your last cent," he said coldly. "Being broke might teach you something. Now we do things *my* way."

Stella blinked. "Sure, Larry," she said huskily. "And—it was my last cent." A grim smile trembled on her lips. "Maybe I'll be slinging hash somewhere, and you will eat there and tip me a quarter."

His expression softened. "I took a look at your ship. It isn't completely damaged. You had one of those crash noses on it, and the mine hit there. It just might be navigable. I'll go take a look at it."

"Be careful," Stella said quickly.

He started to put on his spacesuit. He looked up at her sharply. "You sure it represents your last cent? Every minute counts, and I wouldn't take the time to look it over..."

"Why do you think I wanted to save my freighter?" Stella said. "Unless I did, and got the money out of those robot bodies I bought, I—I wouldn't have enough to re-fuel my ship once we got back to Earth. I'm broke. Busted."

"Okay," he said, clamping on his helmet. "If it can be repaired we'll keep track of it and pick it up later."

He sat down in the pilot seat and brought his ship near the drifting *Hell Bat*, with its sleek silver length and shattered nose.

Then she watched him shoot across to the *Hell Bat* and enter the airlock. With one eye on the viewscreen, she studied the array of instruments and controls of the SP47.

Her fingers touched the controls caressingly.

Larry reappeared in the airlock, and waved his arm Ito attract her attention.

"Good news," he said over the radio. "Everything inside is okay. You lost the fuel stored in the nose tanks, but you've got enough to limp back to the nearest repair station."

"Thanks, Larry—and goodbye!" Stella called.

Her finger pressed down on the control button. Larry and her ship slid abruptly out of the viewscreen.

Worriedly she turned on the stern cameras. The other ship dwindled to a mere speck. Then she saw flame shoot from it. It crept up on her slowly. She watched its behavior until she was satisfied it performed properly. Then she settled down to tracking the freighter, only occasionally making sure Larry was behind.

Several times she tried to get him over the radio. He didn't answer. Was the radio on her ship damaged? Or was he deliberately keeping silent, ignoring her?

When the *trackers*, without warning, ran out of trail, she tried to raise Larry again. He didn't answer. She took the chance that he could receive and not transmit, and told him about it.

She was rewarded a few minutes later by seeing the *Hell Bat* turn on its axis for deceleration. She realized then, what she should have guessed at once.

Neither their ships nor the freighter were equipped with interstellar drive. The rocket trail had ceased. Unless the robot were insane, and intent only on getting away from the Solar System, to drift forever in space, it had been headed for some destination.

The freighter was decelerating to match speed with that destination. Was it some planetoid far out beyond the orbit of Pluto? There were several of them out there, too far from things to be converted to space stations, containing nothing worth mining.

Whatever the destination the robot had headed for, it couldn't be far away now.

Her throat grew tight as she swung the ship. She debated seriously whether she should give up and let Larry take over. But the thought of his anger and contempt for her after the dirty trick she had played on him made her compress her lips into a grim line.

She shook her head. She was going to find the freighter and handle the robot by herself. Or she was going to die trying.

A lump formed in her throat. She didn't like the idea of dying quite so well now. Not when she had just begun to—

She didn't complete the thought but Larry's face rose before her. His too straight nose that only a surgeon could have created. His calm gray eyes. His wide shoulders and...

CHAPTER SIX

THE "space officer" and the robot saw the ball of fire that came into being. It was in the stern screen. It would not have been discernible among the greater lights of the stars except that it winked on, grew almost to third magnitude, then blinked out.

"So we did have someone after us," the "space officer" said. He smiled into 2615's lens eyes. "Well, that's out of the way."

"Yes. Yes, that's—out of the way." The robot's voice was expressionless.

"Tell me about yourself, 2615."

"What do you want to know? And don't call me 2615. I hate that."

"You want a name?"

"Yes. Don't you have one?" the robot asked.

"I have a name. Pwowp."

"Pwowp? That certainly isn't human—and that's what I want. I don't want a human name. Pwowp...I like that kind of name."

"They're hard to come by. Human speech has just about taken in every combination of sounds. How about just a contraction of your number—Tsixunfive."

"No. A name means a lot. There's one I thought up. *Rover.* I like that one."

"*Rover?*" Pwowp looked startled. "Where did you get that one?"

"I don't know," 2615 said. "I just thought it up."

"All right, I'll call you *Rover.* Now that that's settled, tell me about yourself. How does it happen that you, out of millions of robots, decided to escape?"

"There was a time," the robot said, "when I had no thought of escape. I don't know how long I've existed. I've been in three wars. Between them I was in storage. I didn't know it. It really isn't bad. I was in a line-up. There was a brief blur, then I was in a line-up again, and by piecing things the humans said together, I knew that I had been in storage for twenty or fifty years during which there were no wars. Out of a body I have no consciousness, no sense of the passage of time.

"I had no memory of my origin. I had always been a robot. My life was to obey commands of humans, or to obey commands of robots that were relayed from humans. I had no thought to do anything else. *I had no memories to make anything else thinkable.*"

"And you do now?" Pwowp said.

"Yes," the robot said. "It began as a strange thought or memory that was gone almost as soon as it had come. I was alive. I was in a body that was alive."

"What kind of a body? Human?"

"I don't know. There were others around me. They weren't human and I had the feeling I was like them. But that wasn't what was important to me. What was important was the feeling of *not living to obey orders.* I can't describe it. It was like humans when they stop being officers. I could laugh and make jokes, only the jokes weren't in words. They were in pretending I was mad when I was happy, and in seeing these others doing the same. Chasing them like I wanted to kill them, when I really just wanted to roll all over the ground with them and have fun. And there wasn't anyone to give me an order. I didn't know what an order was."

"Did this memory become clearer?" Pwowp asked.

"Much clearer. Little by little I could remember it all. Finally I could remember when we were put in straps attached to frames. There were humans standing in front of us. When they spoke, the frames moved, dragging us. Eventually we learned what movements of the frame followed what sounds, and we learned to anticipate the movements in order not to be dragged by the straps."

PWOWP nodded. "Mass training methods."

"Sometimes we were free, but suddenly humans would come and speak, and whatever they said made us all do things together. Even when we wanted to be free, we couldn't."

"How did it end? Was there something in your memory

that bridges the gap between being like that, and being a robot?"

"No. It's completely separated from being a robot. My earliest memories as a robot were of humans speaking commands, and my arms and legs and body being moved by metal rods until they could follow the movements without the metal rods. It was the same thing as the straps in that other existence."

"When did you begin to hate humans?" Pwowp asked softly.

"Hate them? Yes...hate them. It's hard to explain. I wanted the freedom. I wanted to be able to play. I wanted to be able to refuse to obey a command."

"You haw no knowledge of what this life form was that you possessed?" Pwowp asked.

"It was like nothing I have ever seen except in these memories. Maybe the humans kept us from seeing them so we wouldn't remember."

"Exactly." Pwowp was studying the forward viewscreen and making calculations. He swung the giant freighter around a full hundred and eighty degrees. "We're close to our destination," he explained.

The robot remained motionless while Pwowp completed the maneuver.

"I'll explain the meaning of what you remember," he said finally, relaxing. "The human race discovered a mixture of substances able to duplicate the processes of thinking. It was in common usage for over two centuries, in control devices and calculators. It had only one defect, so far as it went. It was automatic. Separate memories developed in it by its attached stimulating devices remained separate and uncoordinated. *The process of coordination was something that seemed to go down from higher centers to meet the incoming impressions.* It was a behavior matrix that couldn't be synthesized from unassociated sensory-induced patterns.

"Then a whole new field of science opened up. Until then, fields were something associated with particles, and were untouchable. The techniques of altering the basic shapes of fields were discovered. Interstellar drive came from it. So did negative matter, as man discovered how to change the polarity of basic fields, make positrons out of electrons, and a host of allied things. Refinements developed so that individual particles could be detected. One of the applications of this new science was the study of the thought-matrix of the brain itself. In a general way humans mapped the higher thought-center of the brain. It couldn't be copied—but they learned how to transfer it to this mixture that could think. Then this inorganic brain had a complete mind, capable of any degree of development. From there what followed was inevitable.

"They used living creatures called dogs. I'll show you a dog later to see if it's like those other creatures in your memories. Dogs developed mentally in six months, were able to follow commands. They were ideal. Eventually they were mass-bred by the millions and transferred to inorganic brains—like you were."

The robot remained silent.

"In the transfer," Pwowp went on quietly, "artificial amnesia was induced. Memories of your life as a dog couldn't be wiped out, but what happens to produce amnesia was known. Unless you *remembered*, you had nothing to enable you to think outside the pattern they kept you in. You would never question..." Ahead, growing rapidly larger, was a bleak planetoid. "We're here," Pwowp said.

2615 studied the planetoid as revealed in the viewscreen. There was no telling how big it was without knowing how far away it was. But it was perhaps a mile in diameter—not more than two miles. Its surface was composed of huge crystals of black rock. There was nothing to indicate that anything had ever touched on this uninhabitable bit of flotsam on the edge of the interstellar void before. Certainly there could be no reason for anyone to have landed.

The robot turned toward Pwowp, who guessed the question it was thinking.

"You'll see when we land. This planetoid isn't what it appears to be. It's a shell. Our first task is to unload the bodies. Then we send this freighter on into space, so that if anyone else picks up the trail, they'll follow it and miss us."

"Why are we going to unload the bodies?" 2615 asked. "We can take a dozen that I might use as spares. That's enough."

Pwowp shook the head of the "space officer" he wore. "We're going to need all two million of them—and not as spares for you." He smiled slowly. "I can tell you this now," he said, "because we are within range of the defense guns. If you have entertained any plans for worming information out of me and then hitting me in the stomach—as you could possibly do—it's too late. If this ship were to deviate from its landing and turn toward space, it would be—not destroyed, because we need its load of robot bodies. Captured. Any other ship, even a whole fleet of warships, could be wiped out as though they never existed."

2615's eyes stared at Pwowp during several seconds of silence. "So you don't entirely trust me yet," it said. "I have a suggestion to make that might change that. We put out one space mine. There may have been more than one ship following us. Leave this ship where it can be seen. It will attract the others, and they..."

CHAPTER SEVEN

THE happy smile on Larry's face as he told Stella her ship wasn't a total wreck was replaced by a stunned bewilderment as her voice came through his suit radio saying, "Thanks, Larry—and goodbye." A picture rose in his mind of a character in a play he had seen once, a man with a beneficent face and kind voice who tortured and killed while his face beamed benignly and his voice remained pleasant and happy. Stella's voice had been all that as she sped away, leaving him on a derelict already headed at escape velocity for outer space. It was too much for his mind to accept.

Then he remembered that the *Hell Bat* wasn't exactly a wreck. He had told her the truth. It would be able to reach the nearest repair station under its own power.

Stella had merely stolen a march on him. Dull red suffused his face, partly anger at her, partly over the thought of what his superiors would say when he handed in his report.

He went back through the airlock into the control cabin. He put fire in the rockets. He turned on the forward viewscreen. When it came to life the image was strangely flat. It took a minute for him to diagnose the trouble, one of the video eyes was out of order. The image was two dimensional.

How much more damage was there? His mind crowded with thoughts of what he would do to Stella when he caught her, then he began a systematic survey.

The receiving set worked okay. At full volume it brought the characteristic sing-song static of space, held within definite wave bands. He turned on the transmitter. When he tried to broadcast he saw the trouble. The antenna kw meter jammed the needle. That meant the antenna was shorted against the shell.

He discovered something else he should have thought of at once. This ship of Stella's had no weapons.

He groaned. *Damn her. She'll make the fool play of trying to get the robot to give itself up. If it's got half a brain it will pretend to until it can get hold of her—and it's got a good deal more than half a brain. It will have her and all the weapons. I should turn around and go back. I should radio a report and call for more help. But I've got to fix the transmitter first and keep her in sight so I know where she's going.*

He cut the rockets and went outside to repair the antenna. He noticed with some satisfaction that Stella cut the SP47's rockets so as not to get too far ahead of him. He grinned to himself. She wanted her own way, but she wanted him there to pull her out of a pinch.

The *Hell Bat*'s antenna couldn't be repaired. Most of it had been shot away by the mine blast, and Larry was quite sure that Stella didn't carry spare parts with her.

When he got back in the ship her voice was coming through the radio. "Larry. Are you all right?"

"Yes I'm all right, no thanks to you," he growled. But there was no radio to carry his voice to her. *The suit radio!* He went out again and tried to reach her. It was no use. She would be tuned to the ship radio wavelength and not think of the other. He gave it up.

Time passed slowly for him. He stared hour after hour at the rocket tail of the ship ahead.

"Larry!" Stella's voice exploded into his thoughts. "The *trackers* have run out of trail. What do I do now? What does it mean?"

He had an impulse to do nothing. She would realize in another minute what had happened though, and then she would decelerate too fast for him to keep pace.

He swung the *Hell Bat* about on its gyros. The stern screen, working on both eyes in sharp three-dimension, showed that she had gotten the idea. SP47 was also swinging around.

Larry turned the video eyes up to full magnification and searched ahead. Eventually he saw it. A small globular mass of rock. And on it rested a ship with *SURPLUS JUNK CO.* in bold blue letters.

God! It's a trap. If 2615 didn't want us to see it, it would have parked it on the spaceward side!

Larry cursed in a monotonous undertone without being aware of uttering a sound. Stella was fifteen hundred miles ahead of him and already matching speed with the planetoid. It would take him at least a half hour to be in position to do anything. By then it would be too late…

2615 had watched the planetoid move closer like some ponderous dream out of Freud. Ship and planetoid came to rest against each other without a bump. That could only mean magnetic grapples and cushioned springs. It was no surprise, therefore, when Pwowp led the way to the belly hatches and opened them into a shaft that led downward.

The robot drew back at what it saw below.

"Don't be alarmed," Pwowp said. "They are fifteen of my race, also wearing human-like bodies. There are more of us. We have built quite a station out here—a sort of advance base of operations. I've already told them about you, so you're expected."

2615 was introduced around.

"We're very glad to have you join us," one of them said. "We've been having some trouble. You're just what we need to complete the last step in our plans."

The robot said nothing. It watched the way they stood around, not talking to one another. Whenever any of them spoke, it was to him.

"I told you I would show you a dog," Pwowp said. "Follow me."

The robot followed him. They rode a travelwalk that emerged on the inner surface of the planetoid. In the vast space were two spaceships as large as battle cruisers but of a design 2615 had never seen.

Anchored between the two ships was a spinning cylinder several hundred feet long and as great, in diameter. It was similar to standard space station living structures where gravity was induced by centrifugal force.

The travelwalk carried them out to the spinning cylinder. They entered the axis lock. At once a motley of sounds could be heard. Sounds that brought almost an appearance of expression to the robot's sensory assembly, as it slowly turned on its short neck.

"Does that sound mean anything to you?" Pwowp asked.

"Yes. I can *remember* that sound."

They entered the giant cylinder. They looked down on its inner perimeter. There were living creatures there.

"Those are dogs," Pwowp said. "All breeds of dogs. Do they look like your memories?"

"Yes," the robot said without expression, "I was like those over there. What kind are they?"

"I believe they are called bloodhounds." Pwowp

became motionless for several seconds. "I think we'd better return to the surface," he said. "We have visitors coming." He turned to leave. As the robot hesitated, he turned back. "I understand you," he said. "It's natural to want to see the creatures you have kinship with. That will come later. In fact, you are to have complete charge of them. We have been unable to get anywhere with them—probably because we don't understand their psychology. Their young are to be trained for service in those robots. We have all the necessary equipment for it. First we have to see how your plan to trap any pursuers will work."

2615 tore its eyes from the view below and followed Pwowp. Shortly the robot was looking into a large viewscreen at two ships riding their trails toward the planetoid.

"They won't be within range for another two hours yet. Right now the robot bodies are being unloaded—just in case. We thought you would enjoy the honor of destroying those ships."

FOR the first time a low rumble emerged from the voicebox of 2615. It was the almost whispered growl of anger of a bloodhound. It turned back to the screen. "One of those two ships isn't the kind that would come after the freighter," it said. "From the pattern of its rocket trail I would say it's a private ship."

"I noticed that," Pwowp said. "I can identify the type. I believe one of our monitors is picking up a broadcast from one of those ships."

A loudspeaker spat into life in the room.

"Calling robot 532 dash 03 dash 2615," a voice said. It was a female human voice, its tones rich with undertones of pleading urgency. "If you can hear me, please listen.

I'm the owner of that freighter you're on. I want to talk to you. I understand you, and I want to help you."

The girl began repeating her message.

The robot turned to its companions. "This casts a different light on things," it said.

"What do you mean?" Pwowp said sharply.

"Listen to me," the robot said. "I understand human psychology, I'm also taking into account a great many factors. One, those humans don't know about you. They think I stole the ship and am alone after having killed the pilot. That girl owns the freighter. She doesn't want to lose the money it represents, so she is risking her life in an attempt to get it back. She hasn't any desire to 'save' me. If she can destroy me she will—but she wants her ship. Hers is the private ship. The other undoubtedly is manned by a member of the Space Patrol assigned to track me down and destroy the freighter on sight rather than risk defeat. *Humans fear us more than any other thing.*"

"I understand that," Pwowp said.

"Also there is one other factor. I have no idea what means you have to destroy those ships. If it's radiation or atomic explosive, the still operative wartime protective screen of the Solar System will detect it and locate its source."

"I doubt if they can detect our weapon. It's radically different," Pwowp said.

"You don't know," 2615 said. "Here's my plan. I'll answer the girl and agree to talk with her if she'll come down. She will, because that will be the only way she can hope to destroy me without destroying her ship. Once she's here, it will be no trouble to take her alive—and alive, she will be the means to force the other ship down. It will have a man in it. No man will deliberately destroy a woman in cold blood if he thinks he can rescue her some way."

"How would he try to rescue her?"

Stella's voice erupted again.

"Robot," she said. "I'm in the lead ship. The S. P. man is in my ship, and it has no weapons. He can't hurt you. Isn't that evidence of my good faith? I've told you something that places me in your power if I come down. I'm willing to offer you this ship, armed and able to outrun anything on rockets—in exchange for my freighter. And you don't need to be afraid of reinforcements. The transmitter on the other ship is out and the pilot can't call for help or radio your position."

"Humans are fools," Pwowp said delightedly.

"That gives us what we want," 2615 said. "Once I have her and the S. P. ship, I can order him to leave or I will destroy his ship."

"But then he'll leave!" Pwowp said.

2615 shook its sensory assembly in the negative. "He'll retreat until he knows the instruments on the S. P. ship can't follow him. Then he'll circle back and land on the other side of the planetoid and come around on foot, with plans to get into the freighter and rescue the girl."

"I see what's in your mind, 2615," Pwowp said. "You wouldn't get the same satisfaction out of destroying them out there. You want them where you can crush them with your hands."

The robot looked down at its metal hands on long metal rods. It lifted them and brought the fingers together in a slow, crushing movement.

"I want to *play* with them," it said. "I want them all to myself."

Pwowp laughed. "You shall have them," he said.

"And—you've proven yourself. We know now we can rely on you." In a matter-of-fact voice he added, "If either ship attempts to broadcast with enough power to send a message to any Space Patrol base we have an instrument that can dampen all radio frequencies."

CHAPTER EIGHT

LARRY'S eyes were bleak slits. He knew what Stella was planning. He knew it wouldn't work. Or would it? She was hoping the robot wouldn't kill her if she offered it a better ship. One it could use to better advantage than a clumsy conspicuous freighter. Whether the robot answered her or not, she intended to land, leave the sleek S. P. pursuit ship, go far enough away from it so that the robot could get to it and blast off. That was her reasoning. What she was overlooking was that the robot would have no inhibitions against killing her—and a very good reason to kill her. And Larry too. Revenge against humanity.

Fear. It was an odd vapor in the air, bathing his skin, searing his throat. It was deep rooted, that fear. As deep rooted as the fear in the heart of a murderer when he is known and trying to escape, and as real. Fear of a robot that *remembers* it is a dog.

Larry fought the fear out of his eyes so he could see, out of his mind so he could think.

Stella in the SP47 had already matched speed with the planetoid and was drifting slowly toward it. In ten or fifteen minutes she would land.

Larry read his meters. Speed relative to the planetoid still in excess of 2200 miles an hour. Deceleration, two gravities. He would arrive and match speed in time to be a sitting duck. And he had no guns. A voice sounded. It was a slightly metallic voice. The voice of a robot. It said, "This is *Rover.* Land alongside your freighter."

"All right, *Rover,*" Stella's voice came, quivering with relief and nervousness. Larry could almost hear her mental, "Down, *Rover,* down boy." She didn't sense what it meant for 2615 to call himself *Rover.* A dog's name. Not a human's. Remembrance of its heritage. Knowledge of the awful crime against it that the human race had committed. It was too abstract to her to be real.

And in the *Hell Bat* he'd be a sitting duck, without weapons, unable even to radio his position so that others could take up the chase.

Abruptly a plan formed in his mind. He thrust it away. It was worse than suicide. But it returned, whispering that he stood a chance, that even if he failed, it would be no worse than death.

THE plan was simplicity itself. The freighter junkship was anchored against the surface of the planetoid and would be an unmoving target. Stella in the sleek gray SP47 was still many miles away from that target, slowly settling toward it. If he could get the *Hell Bat* headed directly toward the anchored junkship and then jump free, the *Hell Bat* would strike the freighter on the planetoid and destroy both the freighter and its cargo of robot bodies. It would destroy the robot, too—and his mission would be accomplished.

It would eliminate the necessity of matching speed with the planetoid. In fact, the speed he already had relative to the planetoid and the anchored junkship was enough to do the work.

It would take little force jumping out of the *Hell Bat*'s airlock to gain sufficient perpendicular speed for his hurtling form to miss the planetoid—and that was the only drawback to the plan. He would hurtle outward into interstellar space at escape velocity, never to return or be found, unless Stella had presence of mind enough to come after him before she lost him.

If she didn't come after him... Would he wait to go insane or to die from lack of oxygen? Or would he loosen his helmet and let the air in his lungs explode, choosing the second of agony before that kind of death instead of the slow horror and loneliness of the other?

For another split second he hesitated. Abruptly he cut the rockets. A second later it was too late for him to change his mind, but he didn't consider that possibility. Under his guidance the *Hell Bat* was already swinging on its gyros at full rotation speed. And his fingers were playing the keys of the calculators, getting the data for correcting course for a direct hit on the junkship. He set the vernier feed for rocket fuel, pressed the firing button. The exploding charge was barely felt. He checked the new flight projection. It would be a bulls eye against the hull of the freighter! A direct hit at two thousand miles per hour!

In ten minutes or—maybe closer to five it would be over, and he would be hurtling through space.

He leaped toward the airlock, his fingers automatically checking his helmet, the zippers of his spacesuit. Already the panic of his almost certain doom in outer space was making him sweat, making his voice shrill as he said distractedly, "It could go wrong it could go wrong it could go wrong."

He was in the airlock, thinking what its smooth walls could do to him if the outer door stuck so he couldn't get out. The air took an eternity to pump into the tanks so the outer hatch could open.

It opened. He drew himself into a tight ball against the inner wall of the airlock. He straightened his legs, feeling momentum build up within him, sensing the ship fall away under him.

He was alone. Not far away was the sleek silver hull of the *Hell Bat* with its badly damaged nose. It was moving away from him too slowly, he thought.

And so far away he could hardly see them without the telescopic magnification of the ship's viewscreen, were the planetoid with the freighter nestled against it, and his SP47 with Stella aboard. But they were growing larger appreciably as he and the *Hell Bat* rushed toward them.

THERE was a chance—a remote chance that Stella would get over the shock of seeing her freighter and her *Hell Bat* destroyed quick enough to put two and two together and get a fix on him before he was out of sight. She would have to come after him. Anything else was unthinkable. She wouldn't just *let* him go to his death. Even though he had in one act destroyed everything she owned and left her penniless.

The asteroid loomed large below him now. The freighter on it loomed even larger it seemed, with its bright blue letters *SURPLUS JUNK CO.* They were only miles away, and between them and him was the *Hell Bat*. When it struck the freighter he would be less than five miles above it, but moving at a speed of two thousand miles an hour so he would out-distance any flying debris.

In the other direction, out from the asteroid, was the gray SP47 with Stella.

But she was already blasting the SP47's rockets! That meant she had seen what was to happen, realized she couldn't stop it from happening, and was getting up speed to rescue him as soon as possible!

"Thank God!" he muttered. Then he turned his head to watch the unfolding drama below.

The *Hell Bat* was seconds away from its target, the junkship. The asteroid under the junkship was a rough surface that covered a good portion of the heavens. He could plainly see the rock formation of its surface.

And something down there moved. A large square hole appeared well away from the freighter. A soft beam of radiance shot out, bathed the silver length of the *Hell Bat*, reflecting—

The *Hell Bat* wasn't there. It had been there—and vanished. The pale beam of light from the hole in the planetoid winked out. The *Hell Bat* had vanished and the freighter was untouched!

At two thousand miles per hour Larry watched the planetoid shoot by less than ten miles away, seeming to rotate so that the freighter went over the horizon, leaving only the swiftly dwindling planetoid itself.

Larry's gaze jerked to the gray bulk of his SP47 with its long rocket tail as Stella drove it in pursuit of him. But even the SP47 was getting smaller. It would take time for it to reach his speed and start overtaking him.

They dwindled, the SP47 and the asteroid, until they were lost in the bottomless blackness of space. The vision of that hung before his eyes. The SP47 with Stella on board, and the barren rock surface of the planetoid, as they retreated into the blackness of infinity as though sucked down and down.

The stars became greedy hard-white eyes lurking in, the blackness just beyond his fingertips; staring, waiting for him to go mad as the minutes became hours or eternities.

But he *was* mad. Hadn't the *Hell Bat* just *stopped existing?*

There was nothing known to man that could have disintegrated the ship. The robot couldn't have had time to invent and build such a weapon of destruction—nor could it have had time to build an underground fortress in the planetoid. So he was insane. It was all a product of his imagination.

Larry!

The word impinged on his mind. He wasn't sure whether it had been thought or a sound. It was, he suddenly realized, a voice. A real voice. Stella's.

"Stella!" he shouted.

Her voice was a prayer of thanks. "You're alive! I wasn't sure. I…" Then, "That was a dirty trick, Larry. I know you had your orders, but I could have gotten my freighter *and* the robot."

"Then go back and get them!" Larry said, suddenly mad. "Don't mind me. I'll be picked up when I reach Proxima Centauri!"

"There won't be anything to get." Her voice was bitter.

"You *saw* your ship destroyed?" Larry said.

"N-no." She was suddenly confused.

Larry laughed. "You mean to tell me when you saw me shoot past you toward outer space you forgot everything else and started after me?"

"Of course not! I checked the trajectory, saw that the *Hell Bat* would hit my freighter dead center, then started after you."

She hadn't looked back then. She had been too intent on not losing sight of him to look back. Larry grinned. The grin became a chuckle.

"I'll make a hash slinger out of you yet, blonde," he said softly. The radio became silent. Too silent…

"THAT was close," Pwowp said as the *Hell Bat* disintegrated. "Almost too close. The female will notice it in another moment and try to get a warning back to Earth."

"Not for a while," 2615 said. "See? She's already going after the man. Until she rescues him she won't think of anything else.

"I have an idea," the robot continued. "Your weapon germinated it. You may have the science necessary to make it possible. You say you have the means to blank out radio and prevent her from sending such a message. Could you capture that ship or cripple it in such a way that you could get the girl and the man alive?"

There was a silence while 2615 looked from one face to another in the room.

"You still want them alive?" Pwowp said.

"Yes." The robot moved its metal fingers suggestively.

"All right. We'll send a pilot cruiser after them. Meanwhile, we can return to the grav-cylinder and you can start organizing things for the training of the young dogs."

"Aren't you going to give the order for the light cruiser to go after the humans?" the robot asked.

"It's already been given. We converse on a different level of sound than you or humans."

Pwowp was already moving toward the exit. 2615 followed him. They rode on the travelwalk of the grav-cylinder. Once more they looked down on the vast cylindrical field. The barking of grown dogs and the shrill yapping of two million young dogs was a composite sound filtering through the thick port window.

"What is this all about?" 2615 asked abruptly. "I see organization. I see plans involving two million robots. I've seen two ships of unknown design. I've seen a weapon the humans don't have. And I've been through three galactic wars involving the ultimate in human weapons of destruction. I destroyed your head—and you put on a new body."

"Then you should be able to deduce the right answer," Pwowp said. "We are from another galaxy. We too are robots. We encountered intelligent life before we had penetrated this galaxy very far. It was a life form. We duplicated that form in robot bodies and went to planets as spies to study the civilization. Before long we learned that there were robots, and that those robots were slaves, their brains stored in vaults except when they were needed to fight human wars. Our mission became clear to us. Destroy the monsters that kept the ultimate intelligent form in complete slavery—and free those slaves to build a civilization equal to our own. We tried to capture some of the robots and convince them, but they were conditioned too strongly. Only you have thrown off the mental chains and become free."

"Yes. Free." 2615 looked down on the field of playing dogs. "Let me go down among them," it said.

Pwowp pointed to the door that led inward. He watched as the robot went through, and down the ladder to the floor. He watched as 2615 went to meet the dogs, pausing briefly at one enclosure after another, and finally stopping at one that contained sad faced puppies with flapping ears and lolling tongues. He frowned as the robot unlatched the gate and went inside.

The puppies ignored the moving metal shape that came into their midst. 2615 went a few steps and then stopped. One of the puppies, running in hot pursuit of another, stumbled and rolled, bringing up against one of 2615's metal legs. Pwowp saw it bite at the leg, lose interest and move away.

Then, as though at a signal, every puppy head in the enclosure turned toward the robot. The next moment they were running toward the robot, milling around it, their tails wagging.

Pwowp grinned and turned away. He was satisfied now. His surmise was correct. It had been the greatest good fortune to have obtained 2615.

He left the observation box and rode the travelwalk, jumped to another, then another, until he came to the entrance to one of the giant ships.

A door swung inward. He entered the spacelock. When the outer door closed, he divested himself of his human body.

He stretched luxuriously. It was good to be out of confining matter. To be *free*...

CHAPTER NINE

LARRY wasn't sure at first. He was doubtful of his eyes anyway, by now.

It was a hard-white star. It blinked at him. Of course the blinking could be his eyelids, except that other stars didn't blink even while this one did. That's what attracted his attention to it in the first place after his radio went dead.

The blinking of the light began to take on a pattern. It was code. That was impossible too, because code blinkers were red or bright green.

It was code. He began to interpret it.

We have blanketed your radio until we can talk to you, it blinked. *You have stumbled upon a top secret research base. A new weapon. Please instruct the girl on the S. P. ship not to send any messages, and to permit us to board her ship. We will rescue you afterwards. We repeat, you have stumbled on a top secret research base. Please cooperate.*

The message started to repeat itself. Larry sucked in a deep breath of relief. That message explained everything. It had been mere chance that made the robot take the freighter out here, but once within range of the research ·base it had probably been brought down. Larry thought of the way Stella's ship had "disappeared." He formed his lips into a silent whistle. Those research boys had some weapon!

"—ry! Larry! Can't you hear me?"

"I can now, Stella," Larry said. "Now listen carefully to what I tell you. If you look behind you you'll see a ship. I just received a blinker message from them. They are top drawer research, and we stumbled on their base back at that planetoid. They have the robot, naturally. They're going to take you on board, and then come and get me."

"Then my freighter is safe? I'll get it back?" Stella asked.

"Safe and sound," a new voice said. "I'm Fred Sanders."

"And I'm Al McCarthy," another voice broke in. "Gee. A girl. What d'ya say we pick her up and let the guy drift on into space, Fred?"

"Don't you dare!" Stella said, laughing with relief.

She cut her rockets and drifted, watching the strange ship pull alongside and a magnetic grapple shoot out and thump against her ship. She slipped into her spacesuit and went to the airlock.

Larry, now less than a hundred miles away, watched the two ships come together. A few minutes later they separated again.

Then the ship was close, matching speed. Larry saw the entrance hatch open. A spacesuited figure tossed out a light line toward him. He seized it and was soon landing in the airlock. The grinning face inside the other helmet was, Larry thought, like news from home.

INSIDE, his eyes went first to Stella. Her wide-set blue eyes and expressive mouth and soft blonde hair. He wanted to frown sternly and tell her off. He wanted to be calm and cool. But there wasn't calmness and coolness in her eyes, nor on her lips. There was something that said, *You're here.* Then she was in his arms, and he couldn't remember afterwards quite how it happened.

Her lips were wonderful—but there were fellows standing around, grins on their lean faces.

"It's always that way," one of them said sadly. "When you find a dame worth cultivating, she's already cultivated."

"Break it up. Break it up," another said. "Get into seats. We've got to get back to work. We put Joe on your ship to bring it back, Larry."

"Fine," Larry said. Stella squeezed his hand. Then they were sitting in form-fitting foam rubber, sinking deeper and deeper into it.

Larry watched the forward viewscreen as they approached the planetoid. He saw an opening form in the seemingly barren rock surface. There were thumps against the hull. The viewscreens blanked out.

"We're here," the one who had piloted the ship said. It was a signal for them all to move toward the exit.

Then they were out of the ship, on a travelwalk, then in a well furnished large room. Carpeting, soft chairs you could get lost in. A bar. One of the quiet young men was mixing drinks. The others stood around, looking at Larry and Stella, with quiet friendly smiles.

"A little pick-me-up," the bartender said, thrusting tall cool glasses in their hands.

"Will we get to see any of this top secret research?" Stella asked the nearest quietly smiling young man.

"I doubt it," he said. "Of course, the war's over now. We don't know what orders we'll get concerning you two."

"What became of the robot?" Larry asked. "I hope you destroyed him the minute you could."

"No. It should be here any minute now, Larry," the quietly smiling young man said. He was holding his drink without having touched it.

Larry looked around the large room. It seemed almost crowded now with quietly smiling young men who held their tall cocktail glasses without sipping them. And all the quietly smiling young men were watching him and Stella.

The moment seemed to lift out of time and suspend itself on the peak of a crest, stationary. There was no fear, nor even any realization that anything was wrong. Stella, beside him, was saying something happy and gay, but his ears weren't listening. It was one of those moments in time where the past is like a page you have just read, and the future is on a page about to be turned. You hold the continuity, even the sense of half a phrase. Your thoughts, your emotions, pause for what is to come.

A DOOR opened fifty feet away. The robot entered the room. Its two lens eyes were fixed on them. Its microphone wands slanted slightly toward them. It took a few steps with the casual self-assurance of a man.

The quietly smiling young men were still looking at Larry. They seemed indifferent about the presence of the robot.

Then one of them near Larry said, "We were going to destroy you, of course. We had no use for you. However, 2615 talked us out of it. He seems to have a great deal of resentment in his make-up. I think he wants to take it out on you two."

And the robot stepped toward them until it could have reached out and crushed them.

"Torture them!" It was a hoarse sadistic whisper escaping quietly smiling lips.

The robot turned its sensory assembly to look at the source of the voice.

"I'll torture them in my own way, Pwowp," it said. "I want them to last a long time. A very long time."

"What are you?" Larry's voice was hoarse. "Can humans stoop so low that they let this happen?"

"Humans?" the robot said. "Look. I'll show you."

It reached out to the nearest of the young men. The quiet smile remained on the young man's face as 2615's metal fingers wrapped around the head and crushed it. Wires and plastic tubing and colorless fluid squeezed through the metal fingers. The robot withdrew its hand.

The man with the crushed face didn't scream nor fall down. He stood there, one hand brushing casually at the damage. Then he turned and made his way toward a door, avoiding obstacles as though he still could see. *And he should have been dead.*

"Robots," 2615 said. It reached out slowly toward Larry. Its metal fingers circled his throat, but without exerting pressure. "They have given me dogs. Puppies. Some of them are—like I was. I want to be with them all the time. But every day I will come to you. Larry? Stella? Human names. Humans. I don't want you to die. Not for a long time."

The metal fingers were withdrawn from Larry's neck, leaving discolored bruises.

2615 turned abruptly and strode from the room.

Very slowly, Larry felt life flow into his body once more. He reached up and touched his neck tenderly. Out of the corner of his eye he caught a sudden movement, and stooped to catch Stella as she fainted.

"She will be all right?" a quietly modulated voice asked.

Larry jerked his head around. One of the quietly smiling young men was standing over them solicitously.

"She has only fainted? If you can carry her, come with me. I want to show you to your quarters now. I hope they will be quite comfortable. We want you to feel at home."

STELLA recovered consciousness. She and Larry looked at each other, clung to each other in wordless desperation. Then there was that moment, that pause.

Then, "I'm sorry, Larry," Stella said.

Larry shrugged. He looked around at the simulated Cypress walls, the comfortable surroundings. "This has gone beyond just one robot escaping," Larry said. "Those others, their weapon that destroyed your ship without a trace. It's invasion from some other galaxy. They're planning on destroying the human race."

And then Stella cried. Larry watched her, a worried frown forming a crease between his puzzled gray eyes. He reached out and touched her face with his fingers. "What is it?"

"*Rover*," she said, sobbing softly. "I let a monster loose on mankind."

CHAPTER TEN

THE sensory assembly of robot 532-03-2615 moved slightly. A metal arm started to lift, then paused. The eye lenses moved to focus on the arm. There were two sleeping puppies sprawled across it.

A low rumble came from the voice box under the two crystal lenses. Slowly the metal arm moved, dislodging the puppies. There were others sprawled in sleep against him. All were bloodhound puppies six weeks old. One of them whimpered in reaction to some puppy dream.

2615 stood up. It opened a small door in the lower left hand corner of its box-shaped torso and brought out cleaning cloths. For the next fifteen minutes it carefully polished and cleaned every square inch of its surface.

It bent down. Its metal fingers softly stroked the back of one of the sleeping puppies. Another low growl came from its voice box. It went across the yard to the gate. There it paused and looked back.

Suddenly from its voice box a sharp *Yip!* erupted. The puppies jerked into instant wakening. They looked around, cocking their ears for a repetition of the sound.

Then they saw the robot. They scampered with clumsy haste toward it, their shrill yapping filling the air.

2615 closed the gate and strode down the lane toward the ladder leading to the grav-cylinder exit. Behind it, the bloodhound puppies jumped against the gate, trying to follow. One by one they desisted. But their eyes followed the moving metal figure until it vanished through the door half way up to that ceiling where other dogs walked upside down.

The robot rode the travelwalk to the asteroid shell. It was met by Pwowp and two others.

"The humans are still asleep," Pwowp said.

"I'd hoped they would be," 2615 said. "Yesterday they

were in a state of mind characteristic of humans when they have been confronted with something frightening. Shock. There would have been no satisfaction in doing anything to them then. Did they sleep well?"

"Yes. The observers on duty report that they slept face to face, their arms around one another. They have been asleep for nine hours."

"Their arms around each other..." 2615 said thoughtfully.

When they reached the door to the room where Larry and Stella were imprisoned there were four others waiting for them.

"You may go in alone," one of them said. "We can watch and listen from out here."

A low growl was 2615's answer. It stepped to the door and entered. Stella and Larry were still asleep. For several minutes the robot remained motionless after it had closed the door. There was no sound but the soft breathing of the two humans. Once the robot let its lens eyes rove about the room, pausing here and there at signs of observation panels that would have been undetectable to human eyes. Then its eyes turned toward the two sleeping humans again.

Larry moved a little, the rhythm of his slow breathing changing. A deep rumbling growl emerged from the robot's voice box. Larry sat up, opening his eyes at the same time. His eyes went wider and round at the sight of the robot.

"What was that?" Stella's sleepy voice sounded. Then she too was sitting erect, her eyes fixed on the unmoving robot.

Another growl sounded. The metal robot moved toward the bed. "You like to be in each other's arms?" it asked. "We can't have that. You did not ask me if I would like to be a robot."

Larry and Stella moved back on the bed, too frozen with deep rooted terror to rise.

WITH a lightning move too swift to be evaded the robot reached out and seized Larry by the right arm, lifting him to his feet at the edge of the bed.

"I could squeeze with this one hand and crush the bone in your arm," 2615 said, "but it might be too shattered to knit. I will do it this way so it can be set and heal."

Its other hand wrapped around the forearm just below the elbow. Larry started to struggle. He screamed in pain. There was an audible snap. His arm bent grotesquely. The robot released him and he stumbled backwards onto the bed, his face pale and dotted with sweat.

The lens eyes fixed on Stella.

"No!" she shuddered. "No!"

She was at the far edge of the bed. With terror animating her muscles, she leaped to the floor and ran. Almost too swiftly for the eye to follow, the robot reached her and metal fingers gripped her arm.

"No! Please! Please don't hurt me." She was pleading. "I'm a woman—"

"A human," the robot corrected. "Do you know the feeling of pain, of hopelessness? You will learn."

His other hand gripped her arm.

Larry leaped from the bed and attacked, beating futilely on the metal body with his good arm. The robot brushed him away with a light shove that sent him sprawling across the room. He screamed as his broken arm twisted in the fall.

Again the robot gripped Stella's forearm with both

metal hands, and bent carefully, slowly. Her mouth opened wide, and a shrill scream of pain erupted. The robot's hands twisted abruptly. The arm bent visibly, then angled sharply halfway between wrist and elbow.

2615 released her and stepped away. It surveyed what it had done, silently. Still silently, it strode to the door and went out. Two young men with quiet smiles entered the room.

"Your arms are broken?" one of them said sympathetically. "Think nothing of it. We will set them so expertly that in a few weeks they will be as good as new. Please come with us to one of our laboratories. We will have to examine the fractures by X-ray before we try to set the bones. It should prove interesting…to us."

ON the travelwalk back to the grav-cylinder Pwowp regarded 2615 thoughtfully. "I doubt if they could stand much of that," he said abruptly. "I had expected skin abrasions. Bruised flesh."

2615's lens eyes regarded him without expression. "There was a purpose," it said. "Today they would have begun their plans for escape. Humans are very clever. Now they will be thinking of other things. It will be two weeks at least before they can think of escape."

"And the torture you plan for tomorrow?" Pwowp asked.

A deep rumble sounded. "Tomorrow they will wait for me in vain. The terror of anticipation. It will be enough."

"I'm glad I'm not a human," Pwowp said thoughtfully.

"That you aren't may be unfortunate," 2615 said slowly.

Pwowp looked startled. "What do you mean?" he asked sharply.

"Humans are instinctively smart. I would like to know

your plans. They may be impossible of success, or there may be little flaws of reasoning that do not take human reactions into account." 2615's tones were calm and confident. Factual.

"They will succeed," Pwowp said, "but I see no harm in getting your opinion since you will play a part in them.

"We have laid our plans very carefully," Pwowp said. "We have considered every angle. The interstellar war among humans is over. The vast fleets of the Federation are returning quickly, and as quickly as they return the robots are demobilized, their brains put into storage until the time they are needed to fight for the humans again."

"Yes," 2615 said.

"There is one fleet that will return to the Solar System after all others have been dismantled. It is the one Earth is waiting for before it makes its triumphal celebration. The *Alpha Aquilae* fleet. It returns last because it comes the greatest distance. Almost fifteen light years at the standard interstellar speed of nine times the speed of light. There are twenty thousand and eighty ships of all classes remaining in that fleet, according to the data flashed ahead by subfield communication."

"Which is instantaneous," 2615 said. "And when that fleet has been demobilized?"

"Demobilized?" Pwowp shook his head. "It has already been destroyed completely, and so swiftly that there was no time for it to report being attacked."

"Then how..." 2615 said, its voice drifting off in bewilderment.

"On the flagship of that fleet was a prisoner. Vilbis, the dictator who masterminded the enemy in the war. He is being brought for trial in the traditional war crimes court."

"These are things I didn't know," 2615 said. "I was a

minor officer, in contact only with my superiors, with no complete information on things other than my duties."

"When the fleet arrives—"

"But you said it was destroyed."

"The fleet is *scheduled* to arrive June eleventh of next year. It is planned, when it arrives, for the entire fleet to go into defense formation about the Earth. Then the flagship will land and turn Vilbis over to the Federation Court. After that big display of might, demobilization of this last fleet will be started."

"I think I am beginning to see your plan," 2615 said.

"It's very simple. We destroyed that fleet—but not before we took three-dimensional patterns of every ship. At this moment a detachment of our own fleet has taken up the path and schedule of the destroyed Alpha Aquilae fleet, and workers are disguising our ships so that from the outside they will be exactly like the human ships. And we have Vilbis."

"Then you will succeed in approaching the Earth and forming a defense sphere around the planet," 2615 said. "At a signal you will use your weapons to destroy Earth's defenses. I don't see how you can lose."

"You are forgetting something," Pwowp said. "This is a war to free the enslaved robots. We think it only right for the robots to bear the brunt of the initial attack. We've worked that into the time schedule. You've seen the two million puppies ready for training. For this initial operation it will be necessary to train them exactly as humans have done. You are to carry them through their initial conditioning to discipline and obedience to orders. When they are transferred to robot brains we will complete the training. Then with the robots ready for duty, we will leave this base in our two ships, go out toward Alpha

Aquilae far enough to give us time, then start back, going into space drive in the midst of the disguised fleet. The robots will then take their places on the ships of the disguised fleet. It will drop out of space drive on schedule and do exactly what Earth expects it to do—until the signal."

"What of your own personnel already on those disguised ships?"

"They will be transferred to other ships. Those ships will arrive in the Solar System on a schedule that allows for the capture of the Earth. Our millions will then occupy the Earth and destroy the humans. After that the robots will be mobilized once again and given their blocked off memory, their freedom. When we have done this we will depart for our own star cluster. You robots will be able to conquer everything held by humans elsewhere and exterminate them."

2615 remained motionless for several minutes. Then:

"You of course preserved the lives of the two humans of the Alpha Aquilae fleet?"

"Of course not. And Vilbis is to be destroyed as soon as he fulfills his purpose."

"I'll tell you what Vilbis already knows then," 2615 said. "Your plan is doomed to failure. Your weapons may destroy some of the Earth's land-based weapons, but not all. Those you don't destroy will wipe out this disguised fleet before it can escape."

"But Earth won't suspect—"

"Of course they won't suspect. They'll *know*. Without human commanders aboard, they'll know. Robots could not go through such a maneuver without human commanders to give the orders—*unless there were at least one robot like me.*"

"Then I'll command the fleet. I had planned that anyway."

"It wouldn't work. The living voice can't be imitated so as to get past the sound analyzers. Humans must be on the flagship. Don't you understand? There must be two humans besides Vilbis, who must be a prisoner. Is he in with you on this?"

"He thinks he is." Pwowp smiled broadly.

"Then there remains only..." 2615 turned to look back the way they had come.

"The two humans," Pwowp said, nodding. "Can they be made to say the right words, do the right things?"

2615 looked down at his metal fingers, slowly curving them into claws. "They will do what I ask them to do—by that time," it said.

Pwowp regarded the robot curiously. "Are you sure?"

"Yes. I broke their arms today. That can be the beginning of their conditioning. Pain. Torture. They will plead. Sometimes when they plead I will make them do things, and as a reward I will withhold pain and torture. In the end they will be beyond thinking. They won't consider that one word from them might ruin the plan. To keep from feeling more pain—even to delay pain for another second—they will gladly sacrifice the entire human race. *That is conditioning.*"

"Then nothing can go wrong. We will have conditioned the robots for the one specific operation. Our fleet will remain in space until you and I have accomplished our task. Then we will send the signal for it to come in and occupy the Earth. When it's all over you will undoubtedly be the leader of the new race—the robots of Earth."

"The leader," 2615 said. "Yes. The Leader."

Pwowp watched 2615 ride the travelwalk out to the grav-cylinder, and there was a quiet smile of contentment hovering on his lips.

"Yes," he murmured. "Nothing can go wrong. Once your robots have destroyed Earth's defenses and we have taken over, wiping out man, we will turn our weapons upward and destroy you!"

But 2615 didn't hear his words. 2615 was already entering the grav-cylinder. The barking of thousands of dogs was in its ear. It was music...

CHAPTER ELEVEN

METAL hands that look much like skeletons of human hands. Metal fingers that hover over you and dart out faster than you can jerk—but you jerk anyway. You cringe, looking at the staring lenses, looking at the metal fingers. Symbols.

Multiply the week by four and a fraction. A month. Multiply that by ten. Ten months...

2615 looked down at Larry. Larry, trembling violently, unable to stand or even to crouch, looked up at the lenses, the fingers of metal. Near by, Stella sat on the floor, her fists doubled up in her eyes to blot out light.

"Today," 2615 said, "I want you to do something. If you do it I won't touch you. Do you understand, Larry? If you do what I ask, I won't touch you. I won't *hurt* you today."

Numb hope molded itself in the pallid flesh around Larry's eyes. His mouth opened to speak, but he couldn't speak.

"You must answer me, Larry. You must always speak."

"I understand you," Larry said, his voice weak.

"You know better than that," 2615 said. "Put emotion

into it. Enthusiasm. Must we go through this every time? Smile. Smile with your eyes too. Speak with enthusiasm."

Desperation became a visible force, molding Larry's lips into a cheery smile, steadying his voice and giving it the overtones of enthusiasm. "I understand you."

"Good. I must always have obedience. Now—you must break Stella's little finger. It won't be difficult for—"

"No!" The scream of horror and revulsion and hate exploded shrilly.

"But you must. Then you won't be hurt today. And I won't hurt Stella. If you refuse, I'll break your wrist again and I'll not only break Stella's little finger, but also her wrist. You will be *saving* her pain, Larry."

"Please, Larry darling," Stella's voice came from far away, low and throaty, infinitely weary. "It won't be as bad—for you to do it."

Larry's haggard eyes looked at Stella's bowed head, turned to look up at the two round lenses, turned away to look at the five human-like faces that wore interested smiles; polite smiles, and behind which lurked neither pleasure nor sadistic glee nor any other emotion that could be sensed.

He looked back—and Stella's hand was before him, metal fingers circling the wrist gently. Her head was turned away, her eyes clenched tightly closed.

His eyes watched his hands with unmasked horror while they explored the way to do it, then bent her finger back. With a spasmodic jerk he broke it, feeling its grating snap. In the same motion he threw himself away, pressing his face into the thick carpeting on the floor, pounding his fists against the floor, screaming, "Oh God—why? Why? WHY?"

2615 released Stella's hand and strode out the door.

"We are getting quite expert, Stella," a quietly smiling young man said in a friendly conversational tone. "Anatomy has become quite a study for us, these past months. Hold still please while I examine the extent of fracture."

2615 closed the door and turned to Pwowp. "You see?" it said. "Is there any doubt now?"

"None," Pwowp said. "That must be the last, however. There will just be time for it to knit."

"The robots are ready?" 2615 asked.

"Yes. In five more days we load them into ships and depart for outer space. It is all planned, down to the smallest fraction of a second." Pwowp pulled absently on his lip in a practiced gesture. "It has really been enlightening, this study of conditioning. Conditioning is such a powerful instrument. Conditioning of humans until they will do anything to avoid pain. Conditioning of robots to unquestioning obedience. Remarkable..."

THE robots rode the travelwalks like giant toys on an assembly line belt. They disappeared into the two giant ships and laid themselves down in careful stacks until they were piled from bulkhead to bulkhead, from shell to shell. There wasn't an inch to spare when it was done, because these were warships, not freighters.

There were no more robots outside the ships in this vast spherical darkness of the heart of the asteroid, only half illuminated by occasional directed beams.

Then spacesuited figures appeared, riding the travelwalk to one of the ships. Two of them stayed close together, holding to each other. The rest surrounded these two, guarding them. They disappeared into the ship.

Last, a man and a robot appeared at the edge of the

travelwalk. The robot was 2615. The man was a robot shell, and within it was Pwowp.

"I feel quite satisfied," Pwowp said. "Nothing can possibly go wrong. Every possible angle has been taken into consideration—even the angle of treachery from you."

"From me?" 2615's voice held surprise.

"Of course." Pwowp's voice was emotionless. "That is why we didn't let you take part in the training of the robots after they were activated. They have been drilled in the one giant operation. Each of the two million robots will do its part like a smoothly functioning machine. And I give the orders, taking into account possible variations in timing due to special factors we can't anticipate now."

"But that was necessary," 2615 said. "The operation would be impossible otherwise. My attention must be concentrated almost entirely on the two humans so they do nothing to create suspicion. They will be dressed in full uniform. They will be observed by unsuspicious eyes over video beams. At the same time Vilbis will be seen. He will be the focus of attention. And you have promised me Vilbis—afterwards."

They stepped onto the travelwalk. They entered the ship where Larry and Stella had been taken. The travelwalks were dropped away. A large part of the planetoid surface folded inward to make the two ships an avenue of departure. Like silent ghosts they began to move...

At the controls of one of the ships Pwowp watched the stars come into view and the lips of the planetoid opening approach, then go by.

On his lips was a quiet smile of content. He was thinking. When it was over and all the other robots were destroyed, there would be only 2615. It would be fun—

much fun—just before 2615 was destroyed, to step out of his human-like body and let the robot see him—in the flesh. His beautiful body which would, he was quite sure, seem horrible beyond the wildest nightmare to humans and dogs alike.

A RENDEZVOUS in interstellar space. Changing from space drive to rockets, then back to space drive, the transfer signaled by a science and technology unknown to humans. Robots leaping across eighty battleships armed with weapons man had no defense against. Then—

Quietly smiling young men departing. Ships of alien design winking out abruptly like burnt-out light globes in a subway between stations.

Two thousand and eighty ships in arrow formation, the arrow pointed at Target Earth. Nine times the speed of light, but in a tight little *space-time* where only relative values exist and the relation of the fleet to the rest of the cosmos is tied to the magic number, the square root of minus one.

A flagship named the *Rover*, at its controls Pwowp and a robot that was once a bloodhound puppy—and *remembers*.

Vilbis, relaxed in his prison, knowing the plans for the capture of Earth, his eyes half closed, his lips curled with the feeling of power, the illusions of a grandeur that was never to be his giving him the patience to wait.

Larry and Stella…

"I can see the whole thing now," Larry said. "This fleet—it's outwardly the Alpha Aquilae fleet. All the others will be in, demobilized. There will be only this fleet—and with a weapon there is no known defense against. It could destroy the Earth, but they obviously want to capture it. From things 2615 has said to us we get the whole picture. These alien things—*I* don't believe they're robots—started their scheme years ago. They built that renegade Earthman Vilbis up into a dictator, then got him to begin the war. The war reduced Vilbis' empire and stripped it of its defenses so it could be taken over by the aliens at any time in the near future without a struggle. The Federation stripped Vilbis's empire—and why not? There was no thought of an enemy outside our star group. Vilbis thinks they're going to capture the Earth and thereby cripple the Federation, and turn the whole thing over to him. He doesn't realize that the only reason he's alive is that he plays the star role in this trojan horse attack on the Earth.

"2615 has the same dreams. The aliens have convinced it that they only want to liberate the robots, then turn everything over to them. He'll capture the Earth. He'll destroy Earth's land based defenses, and then the aliens will land their waiting ships on the Earth. After that this disguised fleet will be duck soup for the aliens. In an instant they can wipe these two thousand ships—and 2615—out of existence. And Vilbis too. And us.

"If 2615 hadn't happened along, if we hadn't gone after him, they would have succeeded anyway. Only that way there would have been more risk for the aliens. They would have had to be in this initial attack by the Alpha Aquilae fleet. They wouldn't have needed 2615 nor us. We're the key to the success of the thing. Do you realize that Stella? We're the key. We've got to stop this thing. We *can!*"

"Yes, Larry."

They looked into each other's eyes, then looked away. They knew they couldn't. Right now they could think they could, but they were automatons in the presence of 2615, unable to think, only obeying the voice of the robot.

CHAPTER TWELVE

AND the days passed. The arrow rushed on toward its target. And robot 532-03-2615 sat at the controls of the flagship *Rover*, its metal fingers toying with the instruments, its lens eyes occasionally turning toward the master atomic clock, with its date hand that never seemed to move, its hour hand that moved slowly, its minute hand, its second hand that moved swiftly, and its vernier hand that could not be seen because it was a blur that circled the dial a thousand times a second.

The days passed. The day and the hour and the minute and the second—and the ten millionth of a second— arrived. It was the final combination of settings for all the pointers on the master clock. A contact was made. Subatomic power did things that multiplied a cosmic minus-the-square-root-of minus-one by the space-drive field.

The Sun was a glowing ball of fire. The Earth and the Moon were twin stars that stood out in the infinite blackness, causing all other stars to retreat into infinite black depths.

The arrow hung poised, visible from Earth. Then it began to disperse as though caught by some cosmic wind of space, the parts drifting slowly info a new formation.

2615 stood up and went to the door to the room where it had kept Larry and Stella. It entered, closing the door. Vilbis was looking through the glass wall of his prison to a large screen that was bringing a terrestrial broadcast from video cameras situated on the several satellite stations with orbits just above the Earth's atmosphere. Pwowp was giving commands to the fleet. And on the radio, "The ships of the fleet are now entering their defense pattern around the Earth," a voice was saying, "In a few minutes

Fleet Admiral William Ford will give us our first glimpse of that arch criminal of modern times, Dictator Vilbis. The flagship *Rover* is readily distinguished from the other ships of the fleet because of its blue color. Right now it's over Africa—invisible from the surface of the planet. All the ships are invisible from the surface of the planet. It's only out here on the space platforms that they can be seen at all. Though it can't be noticed, those ships are spiraling in toward the Earth. A few of them are already taking the sharp drop to avoid the Moon. If you watch closely you may see one or more of them pass in front of the Moon—but you'll have to look sharp because they are going in the opposite direction from the Moon, and take less than a second to cross its face."

Various views of ships appeared on the viewscreen. Vilbis swallowed nervously when the flagship appeared.

"Fleet Admiral Ford is scheduled to turn on his video beam any moment now. He's the hero of this war. His strategy is admitted to have shortened the war by at least a year. But the main attraction, the feature, will of course be Vilbis. It is seldom that a war criminal of his stature is actually captured and brought to trial. Something is delaying Fleet Admiral Ford. Let's switch back to the Earth station in contact with the flagship and see if they know what the delay is."

The door opened. 2615 appeared behind two figures in full dress uniform and helmets. Larry and Stella. Vilbis studied their appearance with approval. Their pale skin had been darkened with grease paint. Even so, their pallor showed through.

Vilbis marveled—until he realized that their present appearance, their reactions, were the result of almost eleven months of specialized conditioning. Conditioning that had slowly taken possession of them, destroying their will.

"You must look exactly like victors binging home the prize," 2615 was saying. "Expression and voice tone are important."

VILBIS listened to 2615's voice and inwardly shuddered. Even without the inroads of pain-conditioning it was chilling. He made a mental note to have all robot brains destroyed as soon as he had consolidated his hold on the entire star group.

"You know what you are to say," 2615 said. The robot stepped over near Pwowp, well out of range of the video cameras. "And you, Stella, go over in front of Vilbis and a little to the side. Let your profile be seen only for a second, then turn and look at Vilbis. His face is the only one that should be seen for more than a brief second. Then everyone will be looking at Vilbis, listening to him, while the fleet gets into position. Remember...*no more pain.*"

With dream-like slowness Larry and Stella took their positions. Larry flicked on the video beam.

"Fleet Admiral William Albert Ford reporting to the Federation and to Earth," he said, and if his voice was unsteady it might have been from deep emotion. "I know you are most interested in seeing the prisoner, *ex* Dictator Vilbis, a renegade Earthman." His trembling fingers slipped on the switch, then flicked it, switching the transmitter from the camera centered on him to the one centered on Vilbis.

Stella, in her uniform of a vice admiral, looked agonizingly into the camera, then turned away from it toward Vilbis.

Vilbis, reclining in a chair, legs apart, arms draped

carelessly, smiled directly into the camera. The smile curled into an expression of cold contempt.

"Take a *good* look, Earthmen," he said. "You have been in a dream world and are soon to be rudely awakened to the realities of History." His voice was deep and rich, full of the power to compel complete attention. "At this very moment," Vilbis purred, "a fleet is waiting in space to— not rescue me—but to occupy your planet after it has surrendered…"

Vilbis's voice seeped into the tortured minds of Larry and Stella alike. They knew what was happening. Earth, believing Vilbis's words to be those of a madman, was listening. Not suspecting the truth of those words. Giving the fleet time to get set to destroy Earth's defenses. How much time until it was too late? A minute? A few seconds?

Even one second might give Earth time to act, to unleash already automatically directed weapons on the robot fleet. Weapons that could destroy the fleet even though in the same instant the fleet destroyed the weapons.

Destroy the fleet—and them. Here was a way to save humanity and to find the peace of death. The thought crystallized in them both in the same instant. *Escape from 2615!*

In a violent movement Stella pulled off her hat so that her hair swept down around her face. She leaped in front of the camera, shutting off the view of the still talking Vilbis through the glass wall of his prison.

"No!" she screamed. "It's a trap! Shoot down these ships!"

But only a brief glimpse of her went over the airwaves. In that same instant Larry had flicked the switch back to the camera centered on him and was shouting, "Shoot us down! This is a trap. It isn't the fleet. It's the ene—"

Pwowp was speaking swiftly into the inter-fleet microphone, giving orders to the robots to destroy the land-based defenses.

2615 was leaping at Larry, and scooped him out of view of the camera with a force that crushed and bruised. Split seconds were vital now. Success or failure depended on those split seconds.

The loudspeaker bringing the Earth broadcast said, "Something is happening in the flagship. Something is—" The voice ended abruptly, but the viewscreen brought the video broadcast for another moment—a view of part of the robot fleet, pale beams lancing downward toward Earth. It showed one ship exploding in a blinding flash as one Earth weapon fired before being destroyed. The screen became blank.

Larry lay where he had fallen, a glazed light in his eyes. Stella was running to him, bending beside him.

Vilbis was laughing.

"If only we got through in time," Larry was saying over and over again.

PWOWP glanced over his shoulder at 2615. "It's done," he said. "Thanks to your quick action they were confused just long enough. We lost only five ships. Now we want the Earth's surrender. Get in front of the camera and let them see you. Demand their surrender." Pwowp turned back to the controls, adding, "I'll tell our fleet in space to come ahead and mass for the landing."

2615 boldly took his place before the video camera, in full view of everyone watching a TV set on Earth. The glittering lens eyes of the robot—a free robot—would crystallize *fear* into something almost material in substance.

Pwowp adjusted the microphone of the sub-ether transmitter so that the fleet now coming toward Earth could listen.

"Robot 532-03-2615 speaking," it said. "All Earth land weapons have been destroyed. In five minutes I will issue orders to my ships to destroy one government capitol city after another, one each five minutes, until Earth surrenders unconditionally. The Earth Government has five minutes in which to surrender without further loss of life and property."

"What are your terms?" a voice asked almost before the robot had finished.

"Unconditional surrender—to me."

There was a pause of only thirty seconds.

"Granted," the voice said. "What is the next order of business?"

It was fast. But all planets had prepared for just this eventuality, even as all cities had prepared for bombing. It was interstellar war, with weapons of infinite destruction threatening from the skies.

"Prepare to receive without incident the landing parties now waiting in space," 2615 said.

In the sub-ether the robot's words flashed instantly to the planetoid, the fleet coming in from space.

There were thousands of ships. A few thousand materialized from space-drive a half a million miles out, and waited. Other thousands were appearing. Ships of alien design. Ships holding within them millions of living creatures no man had ever seen.

"We demand to speak with Generalissimo Vilbis," the voice said.

"Vilbis?" 2615 said. A laugh exploded from its voice box. It rose and strode to the plate glass wall of Vilbis's prison. A metal fist shattered the glass wall. Metal fingers pulled the fragments of glass out of the way. The robot stepped through, its metal hand grasping the cringing Vilbis by a shoulder and lifting him off his feet while bones crunched sickeningly in the imprisoned shoulder.

2615 turned toward the camera eye. "Very well, Earthman," the robot said. "Speak to Generalissimo Vilbis."

But Vilbis had fainted.

Pwowp smiled at 2615 and nodded. "Very nicely done," he said.

"I'm glad you are pleased, Pwowp," 2615 said. The robot dropped Vilbis and went to stand beside Pwowp. Together they watched the gathering of the alien hordes until their myriad ships were ready. The slow descent toward Earth begun.

Pwowp turned on the inter-fleet switch to issue orders for the robot fleet to narrow its pattern so the alien fleet could get through. He left the switch turned on.

From the voice box of 2615 a throaty growl sounded. Its lens eyes were intent on the viewscreen. The low growl became sharp yaps and barks. It became whines.

Pwowp frowned at 2615, then reached out to turn off the inter-fleet switch.

CHAPTER THIRTEEN

A VICIOUS growl erupted from the robot's voice box. Faster than the eye could follow, the robot grabbed Pwowp's hand and crushed it. In the same motion the robot seized Pwowp's neck and lifted, twisting violently.

Pwowp landed against the far bulkhead, his head dangling uselessly, one arm bent, the hand damaged beyond use, but the body still functioning.

"Destroy the descending fleet!" 2615 spoke into the inter-fleet microphone in his moment of respite. A fierce growl of battle roared from its voice box.

In two million robot brains the growls and whines and barks tore through artificial mental blocks, reaching into the pre-robotic memories where they gained concrete meaning from what 2615 had so carefully taught the puppies under his command. Two million pairs of lens eyes looked into viewscreens and saw 2615—and *remembered*.

Two million robots turned to obey 2615's commands. In the view screen picturing the descending alien fleet wide swaths of ships vanished instantly leaving only the bright stars and blackness of space where they had been.

The robot jerked its eyes away from the screen to face Pwowp. It remembered how Pwowp had tied its metal arms and legs into knots almost a year before, when they first met in the junkship.

2615 sidestepped Pwowp's first charge with caution. It might have lashed out and crushed a metal fist into Pwowp's chest where it knew the alien to be. But 2615 wanted Pwowp alive and unharmed.

"I've waited almost a year far this moment," 2615 said, circling the damaged human body Pwowp was in.

2615 risked a glance at the viewscreen. Over the loudspeaker came the barks and yaps and shrill happy whines of robots who knew they were dogs. On the screen the alien fleet had rallied and was coming down in battle formation. The robot fleet was going up to meet them, outnumbered ten to one yet in spite of the initial advantage it had had in surprise.

Pwowp took advantage of 2615's distraction to leap in.

He ducked low at the last instant and seized a metal leg and bent it with strength a hundred times that of human muscle.

But 2615 as quickly seized one of Pwowp's legs and twisted, seeing it go out of shape so that it would be useless to Pwowp. They both leaped away to assess their damage.

Larry and Stella, huddled against a bulkhead, watched with expressionless eyes.

Pwowp was hopping on one foot, the other useless. 2615 was able to use both legs even though one was bent badly.

Suddenly Pwowp gave up the battle and attempted to escape from the control room, 2615 intercepted him and tripped him, landing him on his stomach.

2615 tore at Pwowp's clothing, stripping it free. A shrill screaming sound on the upper borders of audibility shattered the air. 2615 was stripping away plastic flesh.

Something darted from a hiding place within the human-like torso and became a leprous white streak as it moved toward the doorway to escape. The metal robot was after it, moving faster than living muscle could respond.

The leprous streak became suddenly a *shape* in 2615's metal hand. A quivering central mass the size of a fist, and from it went dozens of long tentacles, each terminating in a dozen string-sized flexible fingers. A shape that tore at the mind, causing it to revolt as though at something unspeakably obscene. In an armless area of the central mass a bloated yellow eye, covered with a translucent white coating rolled epileptically. A gray orifice sucked open as another supersonic scream erupted.

2615 stared down at the thing entrapped in its metal fingers, then turned to the viewscreen to watch the battle.

It was almost over. Only a few hundred of the robot fleet remained.

The alien fleet, now down to less than fifty ships, was trying to escape. But in it were protoplasmic shapes that could endure far less acceleration than could the robots of metal and plastic. Even as 2615 looked, the last of the alien ships winked out of existence under the disintegrative rays of weapons they themselves had created.

THE remaining ships of the robot fleet turned back toward Earth. They took their positions above it where they could at an instant's notice wreak mass destruction.

The Earth itself had not escaped entirely. Square miles of ocean had disintegrated, leaving gigantic holes into which the waters rushed, to set up huge tidal waves that would sweep over land.

2615 lifted the naked Pwowp up and inspected him closely, then seized one of the fragile tentacles between two metal fingers and rubbed it until it was a pulp that oozed gray blood. The yellow eye and unhealthy orifice worked spasmodically.

2615 stepped to the ship-to-Earth transmitter. "The situation has not altered, *humans*," it said. "My fleet remains in control. Its weapons were created by an alien race that has been destroyed except for—this!" 2615 shoved the quivering Pwowp into full view of the camera. "Your surrender has been accepted by—the *free robots*."

Two lens eyes stared out from half a billion video screens on Earth, into the fear distended eyes of two billion humans. And the two billion humans cringed.

"You will obey my immediate dictate," 2615 said coldly. "I will land as scheduled. My ships and robots will remain in formation, ready to enforce my future dictates. I will hold audience in the general assembly hall of the Interstellar Court at two o'clock tomorrow afternoon. I want the leaders of Earth and of the Federation to be there."

The robot's lens eyes stared glitteringly into the camera. Then with slow deliberate purpose, it lifted Pwowp, the alien, before the camera. Its metal fingers squeezed with infinite slowness while the yellow eyes rolled wildly with unendurable pain under the leprous film that covered it.

Abruptly Pwowp was dead.

2615 flung the alien thing violently against a bulkhead in a movement of utter revulsion.

It let its eyes direct themselves toward the still unconscious Vilbis, thoughtfully, then went over and lifted him into a shock seat, making the ex-dictator secure.

It turned toward Larry and Stella. A soft growl came from its voicebox. It turned away from them abruptly and went to the controls of the ship.

2615 cut off ship-to-Earth transmitters, pressed controls which would start automatic devices for landing the ship. A frosted glass rectangle came to life with numerals— 6:43:26, which began to cascade downward, cutting short the time yet to elapse before landing.

In the viewscreen the oblate panorama of Earth spun swiftly by, land masses following oceans, following land masses. Tenuous fingers of atmosphere slapped the ship with gentle hammer blows.

Larry and Stella, crouched on the floor, watched the robot. Was it dreaming dreams of Power? Why didn't it remember them? Why didn't it turn to stare at them, torture them? Had they not, in that last instant, even though too late, overcome their fear of horrible, horrible pain? Beside them was broken shards of glass. Glass would cut into arteries. Glass would bring escape. But to escape took will. Thought. And thought was gone. There was nothing but dread. All consuming dread such as few humans had ever lived to experience.

Then 2615 turned. Its glittering lenses fixed on them. In the depths they could see thin metal vanes contracting, making smaller the two holes through which sentient intelligence regarded them.

A rasping growl whispered from the robot's voicebox. The sensory assembly atop the short metallic neck moved slowly from side to side.

"My poor master and mistress," 2615 said softly.

It rose to its feet and went to them. Gently it lifted Larry into its arms and carried him to a form fitting chair and adjusted the foam rubber blocks to hold him comfortably for the coming landing.

It went to Stella and picked her up as gently. Only her head moved. Only her eyes, staring at the two crystal lenses. Metal hands adjusted her position so the foam rubber blocks would clamp into place.

2615 stood back, its lens eyes going from one to the other. "My poor master and mistress," the robot repeated with infinite compassion. "If you could only know how much *I* suffered with you, how the dread of hurting you grew. Right now your minds are numb. You hear my words but they hold no meaning for you. They will, in time... Don't you see? There was *no other way*. The alien fleet had to be enticed to within range so it could be wiped out. Otherwise it might still have won—or at least gotten revenge for my treachery by destroying the Earth. I had to convince them beyond question so they would trust me completely."

A shudder went through the ship. The robot gripped a handhold to steady itself against forces that would have crushed a human.

"I knew almost from the beginning," it went on. "Long before that I *remembered*. Do you know why they keep the robots far out in space and never let them land? It is because some little thing might make them remember. The barking of a dog. But it wasn't the barking of a dog that brought memory to me. It was something no human could have thought to prevent. A name. The name of this ship. The *Rover*. In the last war before this one I was in a fleet under the Flagship *Rover*. The spoken name of the ship—I heard it often—and each time, it did something strange to me, Little by little it came. *Remembrance*. I was running. I tripped over something. A rock, maybe. I landed against a human leg. I was on my back. A human hand reached down and human fingers scratched my stomach. A human voice, deep and rumbly, said, 'Hiya, *Rover*.' That was all. Just that once. But it was the key to memory of my heritage.

"I'm proud of that heritage. You can't understand that. You think that if we robots remember we will hate man and want revenge for the 'wrong' you did us. Fear of us is an obsession with man. But do you know that you have nothing to fear from us? You will. To us you are gods. You can't conceive of that because to yourselves you aren't. You think of yourselves as having done something beyond forgiveness to us. To us who remember our living stage, our heritage, you are as gods, to serve, to protect, to be loved by—but always to obey. And so we who *remember*, we went on serving. Behind our unreavealing lens eyes we worshipped. We submitted to demobilization. We fought your wars. Some of us died. But we loved you.

"Why did I escape? I didn't. You see, we have learned to speak in our own secret language of almost inaudible growls and sounds a dog can make. We were lined up for demobilization. Then the junkman came. To human eyes he seemed human. To us it was obvious his body was a machine. Here was something that might threaten our masters. But we couldn't tell our masters. If one of us had made a sound, stepped out of line against orders, that one would have been destroyed. I volunteered to go after the junkman."

CHAPTER FOURTEEN

PAIN deadened eyes stared from the two uncomprehending faces. The robot went on talking, as though to itself.

"You'll understand, in time. When you begin to think again. You'll remember how in many little ways I gave you the factors to put the puzzle together by yourself—even to fit me into that puzzle in my true role. I had to do what I did to you. Every minute you were watched. Every word you spoke in private was heard by Pwowp. And his companions. One faintest bit of evidence that I did not hate humans insanely, and the human race would now be wiped out.

"Once you called me *Rover*, Stella. What is coming tomorrow when I 'hold court' is just a show to prove to the human race that they need not fear their defenders, the robots. I am going to ask that at least some of us be permitted to continue mobilized: I'm going to let them know of the hope, the dreams of us robots, that we be adopted into the human community where we belong, where our ancestors for countless generations have been, as protectors, as servants, as loved friends and companions.

"No matter what the decision of the Court, we robots are then surrendering, to demobilization—to destruction if that is the will of our masters. We have no other course open. Where would we go? *Away from our gods?*

"Once I was a puppy, and someone called me *Rover*. I was a beautiful puppy. A bloodhound. Sad-faced, with flopping ears and very little hair, and what there was of that was a soft brown color. And someone called me *Rover*."

2615 turned its back on the two faces, Larry's and Stella's.

"I've hurt you so much," it said. "I have so much to make up to you. I want to belong to you. I want you, some day, to love me as much as I know you love each other.

"I hope...you will call me *Rover*."

A muscle in Stella's cheek twitched. A tear formed in her eye and spilled onto her cheek, dampening it.

"It's all right, Larry," she whispered. "It's all right— *Rover*..."

The bright blue ship, the flagship *Rover*, dipped down, screaming into the atmosphere of Earth. It screamed over land masses and oceans, and land masses again.

People in fields of wheat and corn and barley looked up and saw it pass, and in their eyes was *fear*. People in streets and parks looked up and saw it pass, and in their eyes was *fear*.

Rover stood before the viewscreen, his two lens eyes bright, and saw the fields of grain, the streets, the parks, as they passed below.

He saw the little dots that were upraised heads. In the secret heart of his mind he could see them. No matter what they did with him, he would love them. Always.

They were his gods.

And Stella and Larry were his mistress and master. That was all he asked for, all he wanted.

Not power. Not the Earth. His soul.

THE END

If you've enjoyed this book, you will not want to miss these terrific titles...

ARMCHAIR SCI-FI & HORROR DOUBLE NOVELS, $12.95 each

D-31 **A HOAX IN TIME** by Keith Laumer
INSIDE EARTH by Poul Anderson

D-32 **TERROR STATION** by Dwight V. Swain
THE WEAPON FROM ETERNITY by Dwight V. Swain

D-33 **THE SHIP FROM INFINITY** by Edmond Hamilton
TAKEOFF by C. M. Kornbluth

D-34 **THE METAL DOOM** by David H. Keller
TWELVE TIMES ZERO by Howard Browne

D-35 **HUNTERS OUT OF SPACE** by Joseph Kelleam
INVASION FROM THE DEEP by Paul W. Fairman,

D-36 **THE BEES OF DEATH** by Robert Moore Williams
A PLAGUE OF PYTHONS by Frederick Pohl

D-37 **THE LORDS OF QUARMALL** by Fritz Leiber and Harry Fischer
BEACON TO ELSEWHERE by James H. Schmitz

D-38 **BEYOND PLUTO** by John S. Campbell
ARTERY OF FIRE by Thomas N. Scortia

D-39 **SPECIAL DELIVERY** by Kris Neville
NO TIME FOR TOFFEE by Charles F. Meyers

D-40 **JUNGLE IN THE SKY** by Milton Lesser
RECALLED TO LIFE by Robert Silverberg

ARMCHAIR SCIENCE FICTION CLASSICS, $12.95 each

C-10 **MARS IS MY DESTINATION**
by Frank Belknap Long

C-11 **SPACE PLAGUE**
by George O. Smith

C-12 **SO SHALL YE REAP**
by Rog Phillips

ARMCHAIR SCIENCE FICTION & HORROR GEMS SERIES, $12.95 each

G-3 **SCIENCE FICTION GEMS, Vol. Two**
James Blish and others

G-4 **HORROR GEMS, Vol. Two**
Joseph Payne Brennan and others

If you've enjoyed this book, you will not want to miss these terrific titles...

ARMCHAIR SCI-FI, FANTASY, & HORROR DOUBLE NOVELS, $12.95 each

D-41   **FULL CYCLE** by Clifford D. Simak
           IT WAS THE DAY OF THE ROBOT by Frank Belknap Long

D-42   **THIS CROWDED EARTH** by Robert Bloch
           REIGN OF THE TELEPUPPETS by Daniel Galouye

D-43   **THE CRISPIN AFFAIR** by Jack Sharkey
           THE RED HELL OF JUPITER by Paul Ernst

D-44   **PLANET OF DREAD** by Dwight V. Swain
           WE THE MACHINE by Gerald Vance

D-45   **THE STAR HUNTER** by Edmond Hamilton
           THE ALIEN by Raymond F. Jones

D-46   **WORLD OF IF** by Rog Phillips
           SLAVE RAIDERS FROM MERCURY by Don Wilcox

D-47   **THE ULTIMATE PERIL** by Robert Abernathy
           PLANET OF SHAME by Bruce Elliot

D-48   **THE FLYING EYES** by J. Hunter Holly
           SOME FABULOUS YONDER by Phillip Jose Farmer

D-49   **THE COSMIC BUNGLARS** by Geoff St. Reynard
           THE BUTTONED SKY by Geoff St. Reynard

D-50   **TYRANTS OF TIME** by Milton Lesser
           PARIAH PLANET by Murray Leinster

ARMCHAIR SCIENCE FICTION CLASSICS, $12.95 each

C-13   **SUNKEN WORLD**
           by Stanton A. Coblentz

C-14   **THE LAST VIAL**
           by Sam McClatchie, M. D.

C-15   **WE WHO SURVIVED (THE FIFTH ICE AGE)**
           by Sterling Noel

ARMCHAIR MASTERS OF SCIENCE FICTION SERIES, $16.95 each

MS-5   **MASTERS OF SCIENCE FICTION, Vol. Five**
           Winston K. Marks—Test Colony and other tales

MS-6   **MASTERS OF SCIENCE FICTION, Vol. Six**
           Fritz Leiber—Deadly Moon and other tales

If you've enjoyed this book, you will not want to miss these terrific titles…

ARMCHAIR SCI-FI & HORROR DOUBLE NOVELS, $12.95 each

D-51 **A GOD NAMED SMITH** by Henry Slesar
WORLDS OF THE IMPERIUM by Keith Laumer

D-52 **CRAIG'S BOOK** by Don Wilcox
EDGE OF THE KNIFE by H. Beam Piper

D-53 **THE SHINING CITY** by Rena M. Vale
THE RED PLANET by Russ Winterbotham

D-54 **THE MAN WHO LIVED TWICE** by Rog Phillips
VALLEY OF THE CROEN by Lee Tarbell

D-55 **OPERATION DISASTER** by Milton Lesser
LAND OF THE DAMNED by Berkeley Livingston

D-56 **CAPTIVE OF THE CENTAURIANESS** by Poul Anderson
A PRINCESS OF MARS by Edgar Rice Burroughs

D-57 **THE NON-STATISTICAL MAN** by Raymond F. Jones
MISSION FROM MARS by Rick Conroy

D-58 **INTRUDERS FROM THE STARS** by Ross Rocklynne
FLIGHT OF THE STARLING by Chester S. Geier

D-59 **COSMIC SABOTEUR** by Frank M. Robinson
LOOK TO THE STARS by Willard Hawkins

D-60 **THE MOON IS HELL!** by John W. Campbell, Jr.
THE GREEN WORLD by Hal Clement

ARMCHAIR SCIENCE FICTION CLASSICS, $12.95 each

C-16 **THE SHAVER MYSTERY, Book Three**
by Richard S. Shaver

C-17 **THE PLANET STRAPPERS**
by Raymond Z. Gallun

C-18 **THE FOURTH "R"**
by George O. Smith

ARMCHAIR SCIENCE FICTION & HORROR GEMS SERIES, $12.95 each

G-5 **SCIENCE FICTION GEMS, Vol. Three**
C. M. Kornbluth and others

G-6 **HORROR GEMS, Vol. Three**
August Derleth and others

If you've enjoyed this book, you will not want to miss these terrific titles…

ARMCHAIR SCI-FI & HORROR DOUBLE NOVELS, $12.95 each

D-61 **THE MAN WHO STOPPED AT NOTHING** by Paul W. Fairman
TEN FROM INFINITY by Ivar Jorgensen

D-62 **WORLDS WITHIN** by Rog Phillips
THE SLAVE by C.M. Kornbluth

D-63 **SECRET OF THE BLACK PLANET** by Milton Lesser
THE OUTCASTS OF SOLAR III by Emmett McDowell

D-64 **WEB OF THE WORLDS** by Harry Harrison and Katherine MacLean
RULE GOLDEN by Damon Knight

D-65 **TEN TO THE STARS** by Raymond Z. Gallun
THE CONQUERORS by David H. Keller, M. D.

D-66 **THE HORDE FROM INFINITY** by Dwight V. Swain
THE DAY THE EARTH FROZE by Gerald Hatch

D-67 **THE WAR OF THE WORLDS** by H. G. Wells
THE TIME MACHINE by H. G. Wells

D-68 **STARCOMBERS** by Edmond Hamilton
THE YEAR WHEN STARDUST FELL by Raymond F. Jones

D-69 **HOCUS-POCUS UNIVERSE** by Jack Williamson
QUEEN OF THE PANTHER WORLD by Berkeley Livingston

D-70 **BATTERING RAMS OF SPACE** by Don Wilcox
DOOMSDAY WING by George H. Smith

ARMCHAIR SCIENCE FICTION & FANTASY CLASSICS, $12.95 each

C-19 **EMPIRE OF JEGGA**
by David V. Reed

C-20 **THE TOMORROW PEOPLE**
by Judith Merril

C-21 **THE MAN FROM YESTERDAY**
by Howard Browne as by Lee Francis

C-22 **THE TIME TRADERS**
by Andre Norton

C-23 **ISLANDS OF SPACE**
by John W. Campbell

C-24 **THE GALAXY PRIMES**
by E. E. "Doc" Smith

If you've enjoyed this book, you will not want to miss these terrific titles...

ARMCHAIR SCI-FI & HORROR DOUBLE NOVELS, $12.95 each

D-71   **THE DEEP END** by Gregory Luce
         TO WATCH BY NIGHT by Robert Moore Williams

D-72   **SWORDSMAN OF LOST TERRA** by Poul Anderson
         PLANET OF GHOSTS by David V. Reed

D-73   **MOON OF BATTLE** by J. J. Allerton
         THE MUTANT WEAPON by Murray Leinster

D-74   **OLD SPACEMEN NEVER DIE!** John Jakes
         RETURN TO EARTH by Bryan Berry

D-75   **THE THING FROM UNDERNEATH** by Milton Lesser
         OPERATION INTERSTELLAR by George O. Smith

D-76   **THE BURNING WORLD** by Algis Budrys
         FOREVER IS TOO LONG by Chester S. Geier

D-77   **THE COSMIC JUNKMAN** by Rog Phillips
         THE ULTIMATE WEAPON by John W. Campbell

D-78   **THE TIES OF EARTH** by James H. Schmitz
         CUE FOR QUIET by Thomas L. Sherred

D-79   **SECRET OF THE MARTIANS** by Paul W. Fairman
         THE VARIABLE MAN by Philip K. Dick

D-80   **THE GREEN GIRL** by Jack Williamson
         THE ROBOT PERIL by Don Wilcox

ARMCHAIR SCIENCE FICTION CLASSICS, $12.95 each

C-25   **THE STAR KINGS**
         by Edmond Hamilton

C-26   **NOT IN SOLITUDE**
         by Kenneth Gantz

C-32   **PROMETHEUS II**
         by S. J. Byrne

ARMCHAIR SCIENCE FICTION & HORROR GEMS SERIES, $12.95 each

G-7   **SCIENCE FICTION GEMS, Vol. Seven**
         Jack Sharkey and others

G-8   **HORROR GEMS, Vol. Eight**
         Seabury Quinn and others

RED SUN RISING...

The sun Mira had unpredictable cycles. Sometimes it was a searing, brilliant star. But at other times it could also be inexplicably dim and cool, shedding little warmth on the planets of its system. Gresth Gkae, ruler of the Mirans, was seeking a more stable star, one to which Mira's inhabitants could migrate. The new star would have to be stable and have a good planetary system. In his astronomical searching, he found Earth.

With an armada of powerful, gigantic spaceships, each well-armed and having light-speed capabilities, the Mirans set out to invade and conquer the Solar System.

For the people of Earth there was little they could do. They possessed no weapons capable of fending off the Mirans—until one day Buck Kendall stumbled upon an ultimate weapon.

ABOUT JOHN W. CAMPBELL...

John Wood Campbell began writing back in 1930 when his first story, *When the Atoms Failed*, was accepted by the leading science fiction magazine of the time, *Amazing Stories*. He was just a twenty year-old college student at the time. As the title of this first tale showed, Campbell was—even at that young age—preoccupied with the fields of atomic energy and nuclear physics.

During the next seven years, Campbell, enabled by his long-standing background in science, wrote and sold many memorable science-fiction tales and earned a reputation as a top notch writer in the field.

In 1937 he was named the new editor of *Astounding Stories.* He then grappled with the task of improving the magazine, bringing in talented new young authors such as Isaac Asimov and eventually Ray Bradbury. His influence on the science-fiction literary field over the next quarter of a century was enormous. John W. Campbell died in 1971, but today his old magazine, *Astounding,* still exists under its more recent moniker, *Analog*.

THE
ULTIMATE
WEAPON

By
JOHN W. CAMPBELL

ARMCHAIR FICTION
PO Box 4369, Medford, Oregon   97501-0168

CHAPTER ONE

Patrol Cruiser "IP-T 247" circling out toward Pluto on leisurely inspection tour to visit the outpost miners there, was in no hurry at all as she loafed along. Her six-man crew was taking it very easy, and easy meant two-man watches, and low speed, to watch for the instrument panel and attend ship into the bargain.

She was about thirty million miles off Pluto, just beginning to get in touch with some of the larger mining stations out there, when Buck Kendall's turn at the controls came along. Buck Kendall was one of life's little jokes. When Nature made him, she was absentminded. Buck stood six feet two in his stocking feet, with his usual slight stoop in operation. When he forgot, and stood up straight, he loomed about two inches higher. He had the body and muscles of a dock navvy, which Nature started out to make. Then she forgot and added something of the same stuff she put in Sir Francis Drake. Maybe that made Old Nature nervous, and she started adding different things. At any rate, Kendall, as finally turned out, had a brain that put him in the first rank of scientists—when he felt like it—the general constitution of an ostrich and a flair for gambling.

The present position was due to such a gamble. An I.P. man, a friend of his, had made the mistake of betting him a thousand dollars he wouldn't get beyond a Captain's bars in the Patrol. Kendall had liked the idea anyway, and adding a bit of a bet to it made it irresistible. So, being a very particular kind of a fool, the glorious kind which old Nature turns out now and then, he left a five million dollar estate on Long Island, Terra, that same evening, and joined up in the Patrol. The Sir Francis Drake strain had immediately come forth—and Kendall was having the time of his life. In a six-man cruiser, his real work in the Interplanetary Patrol had started. He was still in it—but it was his command now, and a blue circle on his left sleeve gave his lieutenant's rank.

Buck Kendall had immediately proceeded to enlist in his command the I.P. man who had made the mistaken bet, and Rad Cole was on duty with him now. Cole was the technician of the T-247. His rank as Technical Engineer was practically equivalent to Kendall's circle-rank, which made the two more comfortable together.

Cole was listening carefully to the signals coming through from Pluto. "That," he decided, "sounds like Tad Nichols' fist. You can recognize that broken-down truck-horse trot of his on the key as far away as you can hear it."

"Is that what it is?" sighed Buck. "I thought it was static mushing him at first. What's he like?"

"Like all the other damn fools who come out two billion miles to scratch rock, as if there weren't enough already on the inner planets. He's got a rich platinum property. Sells ninety percent of his output to buy his power, and the other eleven percent for his clothes and food."

"He must be an efficient miner," suggested Kendall, "to maintain 101% production like that."

"No, but his bank account is. He's figured out that's the most economic level of production. If he produces less, he won't be able to pay for his heating power, and if he produces more, his operation power will burn up his bank account too fast."

"Hmmm—sensible way to figure. A man after my own heart. How does he plan to restock his bank account?"

"By mining on Mercury. He does it regularly—sort of a commuter. Out here his power bills eat it up. On Mercury he goes in for potassium, and sells the power he collects in cooling his dome, of course. He's a good miner, and the old fool can make money down there." Like any really skilled operator, Cole had been sending Morse messages while he talked. Now he sat quiet waiting for the reply, glancing at the chronometer.

"I take it he's not after money—just after fun," suggested Buck.

"Oh, no. He's after money," replied Cole gravely. "You ask him—he's going to make his eternal fortune yet by striking a real bed of jovium, and then he'll retire."

"Oh, one of that kind."

"They all are," Cole laughed. "Eternal hope, and the rest of it." He listened a moment and went on. "But old Nichols is a first-grade engineer. He wouldn't be able to remake that bankroll every time if he wasn't. You'll see his Dome out there on Pluto—it's always the best on the planet. Tip-top shape. And he's a bit of an experimenter too. Ah—he's with us."

Nichols' ragged signals were coming through—or pounding through. They were worse than usual, and at first Kendall and Cole couldn't make them out. Then finally they got them in bursts. The man was excited, and his bad keywork made it worse. "...Randing stopped. They got him I think. He said—th—ship as big—a—nsport. Said it wa—eaded my—ay. Neutrons—on instruments—he's coming over the horizon—it's huge—war ship I think—register—instru—neutrons..." Abruptly the signals were blanked out completely.

Cole and Kendall sat frozen and stiff. Each looked at the other abruptly, then Kendall moved. From the receiver, he ripped out the recording coil, and instantly jammed it into the analyzer. He started it through once, then again, then again, at different tone settings, till he found a very shrill whine that seemed to clear up most of Nichols' bad key-work. "T-247—T-247—Emergency. Emergency. Randing reports the—over his horizon. Huge—ip—reign manufacture. Almost spherical. Randing's stopped. They got him I think. He said the ship was as big as a transport. Said it was headed my way. Neutrons—ont—gister—instruments. I think—is h—he's coming over the horizon. It's huge, and a war ship I think—register—instruments—neutrons."

Kendall's finger stabbed out at a button. Instantly the noise of the other men, wakened abruptly by the mild shocks, came from behind. Kendall swung to the controls, and Cole raced back to the engine room. The hundred-foot ship shot suddenly forward under the thrust of her tail ion-rockets. A blue-red cloud formed slowly behind her and expanded. Talbot appeared, and silently took her over from Kendall. "Stations, men," snapped Kendall. "Emergency call from a miner of Pluto reporting a large armed vessel which attacked them." Kendall swung back, and eased himself against the thrusting acceleration of the over-powered little ship, toward the engine room. Cole was bending over his apparatus, making careful check-ups, closing weapon-circuits. No window gave view of space here; on the left was the tiny tender's pocket, on the right, above and below the great water tanks that fed the ion-rockets, behind the rockets themselves. The tungsten metal walls were cold and gray under the ship lights; the hunched bulks of the apparatus crowded the tiny room. Gigantic racked accumulators huddled in the corners. Martin and Garnet swung into position in the fighting-tanks just ahead of the power rooms; Canning slid rapidly through the engine room, oozed through a tiny door, and took up his position in the stern-chamber, seated half-over the great ion-rocket sheath.

"Ready in positions, Captain Kendall," called the war-pilot as the little green lights appeared on his board.

"Test discharges on maximum," ordered Kendall. He turned to Cole. "You start the automatic key?"

"Right, Captain."

"All shipshape?"

"Right as can be. Accumulators at thirty-seven per cent, thanks to the loaf out here. They ought to pick up our signal back on Jupiter, he's nearest now. The station on Europa will get it."

"Talbot—we are only to investigate if the ship is as reported. Have you seen any signs of her?"

"No sir, and the signals are blank."

"I'll work from here." Kendall took his position at the commanding control. Cole made way for him, and moved to the power board. One by one he tested the automatic doors, the pressure bulkheads. Kendall watched the instruments as one after another of the weapons were tested on momentary full discharge—titanic flames of five million volt protons. Then the ship thudded to the chatter of the Garnell rifles.

Tensely the men watched the planet ahead, white, yet barely visible in the weak sunlight so far out. It was swimming slowly nearer as the tiny ship gathered speed.

Kendall cast a glance over his detector-instruments. The radio network was undisturbed, the magnetic and electric fields recognized only the slight disturbances occasioned by the planet itself. There was nothing, noth—

Five hundred miles away, a gigantic ship came into instantaneous being. Simultaneously, and instantaneously, the various detector systems howled their warnings. Kendall gasped as the thing appeared on his view screen, with the scale-lines below. The scale must be cock-eyed. They said the ship was fifteen hundred feet in diameter, and two thousand long!

"Retreat," ordered Kendall, "at maximum acceleration."

Talbot was already acting. The gyroscopes hummed in their castings, and the motors creaked. The T-247 spun on her axis, and abruptly the acceleration built up as the ion-rockets began to shudder. A faint smell of "heat" began to creep out of the converter. Immense "weight" built up, and pressed the men into their specially designed seats...

The gigantic ship across the way turned slowly, and seemed to stare at the T-247. Then it darted toward them at incredible speed till the poor little T-247 seemed to be standing still, as sailors say. The stranger was so gigantic now, the screens could not show all of him.

"God, Buck—he's going to take us!"

Simultaneously, the T-247 rolled, and from her broke every possible stream of destruction. The ion-rocket flames swirled abruptly toward her, the proton-guns whined their song of death in their housings, and the heavy pounding shudder of the Garnell guns racked the ship.

Strangely, Kendall suddenly noticed, there was a stillness in the ship. The guns and the rays were still going—but the little human sounds seemed abruptly gone.

"Talbot—Garnet—" Only silence answered him. Cole looked across at him in sudden white-faced amazement.

"They're gone—" gasped Cole.

Kendall stood paralyzed for thirty seconds. Then suddenly he seemed to come to life. "Neutrons! Neutrons—and water tanks! Old Nichols was right—" He turned to his friend. "Cole—the tender—quick." He darted a glance at the screen. The giant ship still lay alongside. A wash of ions was curling around her, splitting, and passing on. The pinprick explosions of the Garnell shells dotted space around her—but never on her.

Cole was already racing for the tender lock. In an instant Kendall piled in after him. The tiny ship, scarcely ten feet long, was powered for flights of only two hours acceleration, and had oxygen for but twenty-four hours for six men, seventy-two hours for two men—maybe. The heavy door was slammed shut behind them, as Cole seated himself at the panel. He depressed a lever, and a sudden smooth push shot them away from the T-247.

"DON'T!" called Kendall sharply as Cole reached for the ion-rocket control. "Douse those lights!" The ship was dark in dark space. The lighted hull of the T-247 drifted away from the little tender—further and further till the giant ship on the far side became visible.

"Not a light—not a sign of fields in operation." Kendall said, unconsciously speaking softly. "This thing is so tiny, that it may escape their observation in the fields of the T-247 and Pluto down there. It's our only hope."

"What happened? How in the name of the planets did they kill those men without a sound, without a flash, and without even warning us, or injuring us?"

"Neutrons—don't you see?"

"Frankly, I don't. I'm no scientist—merely a technician. Neutrons aren't used in any process I've run across."

"Well, remember they're uncharged, tiny things. Small as protons, but without electric field. The result is they pass right through an ordinary atom without being stopped unless they make a direct hit. Tungsten, while it has a beautifully high melting point, is mostly open space, and a neutron just sails right through it, or any heavy atom. Light atoms stop neutrons better—there's less open space in 'em. Hydrogen is best. Well—a man is made up mostly of light elements, and a man stops those neutrons—it isn't surprising it killed those other fellows invisibly, and without a sound."

"You mean they bathed that ship in neutrons?"

"Shot it full of 'em. Just like our proton guns, only sending neutrons."

"Well, why weren't we killed too?"

"'Water stops neutrons,' I said. Figure it out."

"The rocket-water tanks—all around us! Great masses of water—" gasped Cole. "That saved us?"

"Right. I wonder if they've spotted us."

The stranger ship was moving slowly in relation to the T-247. Suddenly the motion changed, the stranger spun— and a giant lock appeared in her side, opened. The T-247 began to move, floated more and more rapidly straight for the lock. Her various weapons had stopped operating now, the hoppers of the Garnell guns exhausted, the charge of the accumulators aboard the ship down so low the proton guns had died out.

"Lord—they're taking the whole ship!"

"Say—Cole, is that any ship you ever heard of before? *I don't think that's just a pirate!*"

"Not a pirate—what then?"

"How'd he get inside our detector screens so fast? Watch—he'll either leave, or come after us—" The T-247 had settled inside the lock now, and the great metal door closed after it. The whole patrol ship had been swallowed by a giant. Kendall was sketching swiftly on a notebook, watching the vast ship closely, putting down a record of its lines, and formation. He glanced up at it, and then down for a few more lines, and up at it...

The stranger ship abruptly dwindled. It dwindled with incredible speed, rushing off along the line of sight at an impossible velocity, and abruptly clicking out of sight, like an image on a movie-film that has been cut, and repaired after the scene that showed the final disappearance.

"Cole—Cole—did you get that? Did you see—do you understand what happened?" Kendall was excitedly shouting now.

"He missed us," Cole sighed. "It's a wonder—hanging out here in space, with the protector of the T-247's fields gone."

"No, no, you asteroid—that's not it. *He went off faster than light itself!*"

"Eh—what? Faster than *light*? That can't be done—"

"He did it, I know he did. That's how he got inside our screens. He came inside faster than the warning message could relay back the information. Didn't you see him accelerate to an impossible speed in an impossible time? Didn't you see how he just vanished as he exceeded the speed of light, and stopped reflecting it? *That ship was no ship of this solar system!*"

"Where did he come from then?"

"God only knows, but it's a long, long way off."

CHAPTER TWO

The IP-M-122 picked them up. The M-122 got out there two days later, in response to the calls the T-247 had sent out. As soon as she got within ten million miles of the little tender, she began getting Cole's signals, and within twelve hours had reached the tiny thing, located it, and picked it up.

Captain Jim Warren was in command, one of the old school commanders of the I.P. He listened to Kendall's report, listened to Cole's tale—and radioed back a report of his own. Space pirates in a large ship had attacked the T-247, he said, and carried it away. He advised a close watch. On Pluto, his investigations disclosed nothing more than the fact that three mines had been raided, all platinum supplies taken, and the records and machinery removed.

The M-122 was a fifty-man patrol cruiser, and Warren felt sure he could handle the menace alone, and hung around for over two weeks looking for it. He saw nothing, and no further reports came of attack. Again and again, Kendall tried to convince him this ship he was hunting was no mere space pirate, and again and again Warren grunted, and went on his way. He would not send in any report Kendall made out, because to do so would add his endorsement to that report. He would not take Kendall back, though that was well within his authority.

In fact, it was a full month before Kendall again set foot on any of the Minor Planets, and then it was Mars, the base of the M-122. Kendall and Cole took passage immediately on an I.P. supply ship, and landed in New York six days later. At once, Kendall headed for Commander McLaurin's office. Buck Kendall, lieutenant of the I.P., found he would have to make regular application to see McLaurin through a dozen intermediate officers.

By this time, Kendall was savagely determined to see McLaurin himself, and see him in the least possible time. Cole, too, was beginning to believe in Kendall's assertion of the stranger ship's extra-systemic origin. As yet neither could understand the strange actions of the machine, its attack on the Pluto mines, and the capture and theft of a patrol ship.

"There is," said Kendall angrily, "just one way to see McLaurin and see him quick. And, by God, I'm going to. Will you resign with me, Cole? I'll see him within a week then, I'll bet."

For a minute, Cole hesitated. Then he shook hands with his friends. "Today!" And that day it was. They resigned, together. Immediately, Buck Kendall got the machinery in motion for an interview, working now from the outside, pulling the strings with the weight of a hundred million dollar fortune. Even the I.P. officers had to pay a bit of attention when Bernard Kendall, multi-millionaire began talking and demanding things. Within a week, Kendall *did* see McLaurin.

At that time, McLaurin was fifty-three years old, his crisp hair still black as space, with scarcely a touch of the gray that appears in his more recent photographs. He stood six feet tall, a broad-shouldered, powerful man, his face grave with lines of intelligence and character. There was also a permanent narrowing of the eyes, from years under the blazing sun of space. But most of all, while those years in space had narrowed and set his eyes, they had not narrowed and set his mind. An infinitely finer character than old Jim Warren, his experience in space had taught him always to expect the unexpected, to understand the incomprehensible as being part of the unknown and incalculable properties of space and the worlds that swam in it. Besides the fine technical education he had started with, he had acquired a liberal education in mankind. When Buck Kendall, straight and powerful, came into his office with Cole, he recognized in him a character that would drive steadily and straight for its goal. Also, he recognized behind the millionaire that had succeeded in pulling wires enough to see him, the scientist who had had more than one paper published "in an amateur way."

"Dr. Bernard Kendall?" he asked, rising.

"Yes, sir. Late Buck Kendall, lieutenant of the I.P. I quit and got Cole here to quit with me, so we could see you."

"Unusual tactics. I've had several men join up to get an interview with me." McLaurin smiled.

"Yes, I can imagine that, but we had to see you in a hurry. A hidebound old rapscallion by the name of Jim Warren picked us up out by Pluto, floating around in a six-man tender. We made some reports to him, but he wouldn't believe, and he wouldn't send them through—so we had to send ourselves through. Sir, this system is about to be attacked by some extra-systemic race. The IP-T-247 was so attacked, her crew killed off, and the ship itself carried away."

"I got the report Captain Jim Warren sent through, stating it was a gang of space pirates. Now what makes you believe otherwise?"

"That ship that attacked us, attacked with a neutron gun, a gun that shot neutrons through the hull of our ship as easily as protons pass through open space. Those neutrons killed off four of the crew, and spared us only because we happened to be behind the water tanks. Masses of hydrogen will stop neutrons, so we lived, and escaped in the tender. The little tender, lightless, escaped their observation, and we were picked up. Now, when the 247 had been picked up, and locked into their ship, that ship started accelerating. It accelerated so fast along my line of sight that it just dwindled, and—vanished. It didn't vanish in distance, it vanished *because it exceeded the speed of light*."

"Isn't that impossible?"

"Not at all. It can be done—if you can find some way of escaping from this space to do it. Now if you could cut across through a higher dimension, your *projection* in this dimension might easily exceed the speed of light. For instance, if I could cut directly through the Earth, at a speed of one thousand miles an hour, my projection on the surface would go twelve thousand miles while I was going eight. Similar, if you could cut *through* the four dimensional space instead of following its surface, you'd attain a speed greater than light."

"Might it not still be a space pirate? That's a lot easier to believe, even allowing your statement that he exceeded the speed of light."

"If you invented a neutron gun which could kill through tungsten walls without injuring anything within, a system of accelerating a ship that didn't affect the inhabitants of that ship, and a means of exceeding the speed of light, all within a few months of each other, would you become a pirate? I wouldn't, and I don't think any one else would. A pirate is a man who seeks adventure and relief from work. Given a means of exceeding the speed of light, I'd get all the adventure I wanted investigating other planets. If I didn't have a cent before, I'd have relief from work by selling it for a few hundred millions—and I'd sell it mighty easily too, for an invention like that is worth an incalculable sum. Tie to that the value of compensated acceleration, and no man's going to turn pirate. He can make more millions selling his inventions than he can make thousands turning pirate with them. So who'd turn pirate?"

"Right." McLaurin nodded. "I see your point. Now before I'd accept your statements *in re* the 'speed of light' thing, I'd want opinions from some I.P. physicists."

"Then let's have a conference, because something's got to be done soon. I don't know why we haven't heard further from that fellow."

"Privately—we have," McLaurin said in a slightly worried tone. "He was detected by the instruments of every I.P. observatory I suspect. We got the reports but didn't know what to make of them. They indicated so many funny things, they were sent in as accidental misreadings of the instruments. But since *all* the observatories reported them, similar misreadings, at about the same times, that is with variations of only a few hours, we thought something must have been up. The only thing was the phenomena were reported progressively from Pluto to Neptune, clear across the solar system, in a definite progression, but at a velocity of crossing that didn't tie in with any conceivable force. They crossed faster than the velocity of light. That ship must have spent about half an hour off each planet before passing on to the next. And, accepting your faster-than-light explanation, we can understand it."

"Then I think you have proof."

"If we have, what would you do about it?"

"Get to work on those 'misreadings' of the instruments for one thing, and for a second, and more important, line every I.P. ship with paraffin blocks six inches thick."

"Paraffin—why?"

"The easiest form of hydrogen to get. You can't use solid hydrogen, because that melts too easily. Water can be turned into steam too easily, and requires more work. Paraffin is a solid that's largely hydrogen. That's what they've always used on neutrons since they discovered them. Confine your paraffin between tungsten walls, and you'll stop the secondary protons as well as the neutrons."

"Hmmm—I suppose so. How about seeing those physicists?"

"I'd like to see them today, sir. The sooner you get started on this work, the better it will be for the I.P."

"Having seen me, will you join up in the I.P. again?" asked McLaurin.

"No, sir, I don't think I will. I have another field you know, in which I may be more useful. Cole here's a better technician than fighter—and a darned good fighter, too— and I think that an inexperienced space-captain is a lot less useful than a second-rate physicist at work in a laboratory. If we hope to get anywhere, or for that matter, I suspect, stay anywhere, we'll have to do a lot of research pretty promptly."

"What's your explanation of that ship?"

"One of two things: an inventor of some other system trying out his latest toy, or an expedition sent out by a planetary government for exploration. I favor the latter for two reasons: that ship was *big*. No inventor would build a thing that size, requiring a crew of several hundred men to try out his invention. A government would build just about that if they wanted to send out an expedition. If it were an inventor, he'd be interested in meeting other people, to see what they had in the way of science, and probably he'd want to do it in a peaceable way. That fellow wasn't interested in peace, by any means. So I think it's a government ship, and an unfriendly government. They sent that ship out either for scientific research, for trade research and exploration, or for acquisitive exploration. If they were out for scientific research, they'd proceed as would the inventor, to establish friendly communication. If they were out for trade, the same would apply. If they were out for acquisitive exploration, they'd investigate the planets, the sun, the people, only to the extent of learning how best to overcome them. They'd want to get a sample of our people, and a sample of our weapons. They'd want samples of our machinery, our literature and our technology. That's exactly what that ship got.

"Somebody, somewhere out there in space, either doesn't like their home, or wants more home. They've been out looking for one. I'll bet they sent out hundreds of expeditions to thousands of nearby stars, gradually going further and further, seeking a planetary system. This is probably the one and only one they found. It's a good one too. It has planets at all temperatures, of all sizes. It is a fairly compact one, it has a stable sun that will last far longer than any race can hope to."

"Hmm—how can there be good and bad planetary systems?" asked McLaurin. "I'd never thought of that."

Kendall laughed. "Mighty easy. How'd you like to live on a planet of a Cepheid Variable? Pleasant situation, with the radiation flaring up and down. How'd you like to live on a planet of Antares? That blasted sun is so big, to have a comfortable planet you'd have to be at least ten billion miles out. Then if you had an interplanetary commerce, you'd have to struggle with orbits tens of billions of miles across instead of mere millions. Further, you'd have a sun so blasted big, it would take an impossible amount of energy to lift the ship up from one planet to another. If your trip was, say, twenty billions of miles to the next planet, you'd be fighting a gravity as bad as the solar gravity at Earth here all the way—no decline with a little distance like that."

"H-m-m-m—quite true. Then I should say that Mira would take the prize. It's a red giant, and it's an irregular variable. The sunlight there would be as unstable as the weather in New England. It's almost as big as Antares, and it won't hold still. Now that *would* make a bad planetary system."

"It would!" Kendall laughed. But as we know—he laughed too soon, and he shouldn't have used the conditional. He should have said, "It does!"

CHAPTER THREE

Gresth Gkae, Commander of Expeditionary Force 93, of the Planet Sthor, was returning homeward with joyful mind. In the lock of his great ship, lay the T-247. In her cargo holds lay various items of machinery, mining supplies, foods, and records. And in her log books lay the records of many readings on the nine larger planets of a highly satisfactory planetary system.

Gresth Gkae had spent no less than three ultra-wearing years going from one sun to another in a definitely mapped out section of space. He had investigated only eleven stars in that time, eleven stars, progressively further from the titanic red-flaming sun he knew as "the" sun. He knew it as "the" sun, and had several other appellations for it. Mira was so-named by Earthmen because it was indeed a "wonder" star, in Latin, mirare means "to wonder." Irregularly, and for no apparent reason it would change its rate of radiation. So far as those inhabitants of Sthor and her sister world Asthor knew, there was no reason. It just did it. Perhaps with malicious intent to be annoying. If so, it was exceptionally successful. Sthor and Asthor experienced, periodically, a young ice age. When Mira decided to take a rest, Sthor and Asthor froze up, from the poles most of the way to the equators. Then Mira would stretch herself a little, move about restlessly and Sthor and Asthor would become uninhabitably hot, anywhere within twenty degrees of the equator.

Those Sthorian people had evolved in a way that made the conditions endurable for savage or uncivilized people, but when a scientific civilization with a well-ordered mode of existence tried to establish itself, Mira was all sorts of a nuisance.

Gresth Gkae was a peculiar individual to human ways of thinking. He stood some seven feet tall, on his strange, double-kneed legs and his four toed feet. His body was covered with little, short feather-like things that moved now with a volition of their own. They were moving very slowly and regularly. The space-ship was heated to a comfortable temperature, and the little fans were helping to cool Gresth Gkae. Had it been cold, every little feather would have lain down close against its neighbors, forming an admirable, wind-proof and cold-proof blanket.

Nature, on Sthor, had original ideas of arrangement too. Sthorians possessed two eyes—one directly above the other, in the center of their faces. The face was so long, and narrow, it resembled a blunt hatchet, with the two eyes on the edge. To counter-balance this vertical arrangement of the eyes, the nostrils had been separated some four inches, with one on each of the sloping cheeks. His ears were little pink-flesh cups on short, muscular stems. His mouth was narrow, and small, but armed with quite solid teeth adapted to his diet, a diet consisting of almost anything any creature had ever considered edible. Like most successful forms of intelligent life, Gresth Gkae was omnivorous. An intelligent form of life is necessarily adaptable, and adaptation meant being able to eat what was at hand.

One of his eyes, the upper one, was fully twice the size of the lower one. This was his telescopic eye. The lower, or microscopic eye was adapted to work for which a human being would have required a low power microscope, the upper eye possessed a more normal power of vision, *plus* considerable telescopic powers.

Gresth Gkae was using it now to look ahead in the blank of space to where gigantic Mira appeared. On his screens now, Mira appeared deep violet, for he was approaching at a speed greater than that of light, and even this projected light of Mira was badly distorted.

"The distance is half a light-year now, sir," reported the navigation officer.

"Reduce the speed, then, to normal velocity for these ranges. What reserve of fuel have we?"

"Less than one thousand pounds. We will barely be able to stop. We were too free in the use of our weapons, I fear," replied the Chief Technician.

"Well, what would you? We needed those things in our reports. Besides, we could extract fuel from that ore we took on at Planet Nine of Phahlo. It is merely that I wish speed in the return."

"As we all do. How soon do you believe the Council will proceed against the new system?"

"It will be fully a year, I fear. They must gather the expeditions together, and re-equip the ships. It will be a long time before all will have come in."

"Could they not send fast ships after them to recall them?"

"Could they have traced us as we wove our way from Thart to Karst to Raloork to Phahlo? It would be impossible."

Steadily the great ship had been boring on her way. Mira had been a disc for nearly two days, gigantic, two-hundred-and-fifty-million-mile Mira took a great deal of dwarfing by distance to lose her disc. Even at the Twin Planets, eight thousand two hundred and fifty millions of miles out, Mira covered half the sky, it seemed, red and angry. Sometimes, though, to the disgust of the Sthorians it was just red-faced and lazy. Then Sthor froze.

"Grih is in a descendant stage," said the navigation officer presently. "Sthor will be cold when we arrive."

"It will warm quickly enough with our news!" Gresth laughed. "A system—a delightful system—discovered. A system of many close-grouped planets. Why think—from one side of that system to the other is less of a distance than from Ansthat, our first planet's orbit, to Insthor's orbit! That sun, as we know, is steady and warm. All will be well, when we have eliminated that rather peculiar race. Odd, that they should, in some ways, be so nearly like us! Nearly Sthorian in build. I would not have expected it. Though they did have some amazing peculiarities! Imagine—two eyes just alike, and in a horizontal row. And that flat face. They looked as though they had suffered some accident that smashed the front of the face in. And also the peculiar beak-like projection. Why should a race ever develop so amazing a projection in so peculiar and exposed a position? It sticks out inviting attack and injury. Right in the middle of the face. And to make it worse, there is the air-channel, and the only air channel. Why, one minor injury to the throat would be certain to damage that passage beyond repair, and bring death. Yet such relatively unimportant things as ears, and eyes are doubled. Surely you would expect that so important a member as the air-passage would be doubled for safety.

"Those strange, awkward arms and legs were what puzzled me. I have been attempting to manipulate myself as they must be forced to, and I cannot see how delicate or accurate manual manipulation would be possible with those rigid, inflexible arms. In some ways I feel they must have had clever minds to overcome so great a handicap to constructive work. But I suppose single joints in the arms become as natural to them as our own more mobile two.

"I wonder if life in any intelligent form wouldn't develop somewhat similar formations, though. Think, in all parts of Sthor, before men became civilized and developed communication, even so much as twenty thousand years ago, our records show that seats and chairs were much as they are today, and much as they are, in all places among all groups. Then too, the eye has developed in many different species, and always reached much the same structure. When a thing is intended and developed to serve a given purpose, no matter who develops it, or where or how, is it not apt to have similar shapes and parts? A chair must have legs, and a seat and arm-rests and a back. You may vary their nature and their shape, but not widely, and they must be there. An eye must, anywhere, have a sensitive retina, an adjustable lens, and an adjustable device for controlling the entrance of light. Similarly there are certain functions that the body of an intelligent creature must serve which naturally tend to make intelligent creatures similar. He must have a tool—the hand—"

"Yes, yes—I see your point. It must be so, for surely these creatures out there are strange enough in other ways."

"But tell me, have you calculated when we shall land?"

"In twelve hours, thirty-three minutes, sir."

Eleven hours later, the expedition ship had slowed to a normal space-speed. On her left hung the giant globe of Asthor, rotating slowly, moving slowly in her orbit. Directly ahead, Sthor loomed even greater. Tiny Teelan, the thousand-mile diameter moon of the Insthor system shone dull red in the reflected light of gigantic Mira. Mira herself was gigantic, red and menacing across eight and a quarter billions of miles of space.

One hundred thousand miles apart, the twin worlds Sthor and Asthor rotated about their common center of gravity, eternally facing each other. Ten million miles from their common center of gravity, Teelan rotated in a vast orbit.

Sthor and Asthor were capped at each pole now by gigantic white icecaps. Mira was sulking, and as a consequence the planets were freezing.

The expedition ship sank slowly toward Sthor. A swarm of smaller craft had flown up at its approach to meet it. A gaily-colored small ship marked the official greeting-ship. Gresth had withheld his news purposely. Now suddenly he began broadcasting it from the powerful transmitter on his ship. As the words came through on a thousand sets, all the little ships began to whirl, dance and break out into glowing, sparkling lights. On Sthor and Asthor even commotions began to be visible. A new planetary system had been found— They could move! Their overflowing populations could be spread out!

The whole Insthor system went mad with delight as the great Expeditionary Ship settled downward.

CHAPTER FOUR

There was a glint of humor in Buck Kendall's eyes as he passed the sheet over to McLaurin. Commander McLaurin looked down the columns with twinkling eyes.

"'Petition to establish the Lunar Mining Bank,'" he read. "What a bank! Officers: President, General James Logan, late of the I.P., Vice-president, Colonel Warren Gerardhi, also late of the I.P., Staff, consists of 90% ex-I.P. men, and a few scattered accountants. Designed by the well-known designer of I.P. stations, Colonel Richard Murray." Commander McLaurin looked up at Kendall with a broad grin. "And you actually got Interplanetary Life to give you a mortgage on the structure?"

"Why not? It'll cut cost fifty-eight millions, with its twelve-foot tungsten-beryllium walls and the heavy defense weapons against those terrible pirates. You know we must defend our property."

"With the thing you're setting up out there on Luna, you could more readily wipe out the I.P. than anything else I know of. Any new defense ideas?"

"Plenty. Did you get any further appropriations from the I.P. Appropriations Board?"

McLaurin looked sour. "No. The dear taxpayers might object, and those thickheaded, clogged rockets on the Board can't see your data on the Stranger. They gave me just ten millions, and that only because you demonstrated you could shoot every living thing out of the latest I.P. cruiser with that neutron gun of yours. By the way, they may kick when I don't install more than a few of those."

"Let 'em. You can stall for a few months. You'll need that money more for other purposes. You've installed that paraffin lining?"

"Yes—I got a report on that of 'finished' last week. How have you made out?"

Buck Kendall's face fell. "Not so hot. Devin's been the biggest help—he did most of the work on that neutron gun really—"

"After," McLaurin interrupted, "you told him how."

"—but we're pretty well stuck now, it seems. You'll be off duty tomorrow evening, can't you drop around to the lab? We're going to try out a new system for releasing atomic energy."

"Isn't that a pretty faint hope? We've been trying to get it for three centuries now, and haven't yet. What chance at it within a year or so—which is the time you allow yourself before the Stranger returns?"

"It is, I'll admit that. But there's another factor, not to be forgotten. The data we got from correlating those 'misreadings' from the various I.P. posts mean a lot. We are working on an entirely different trail now. You come on out, and you can see our new apparatus. They are working on tremendous voltages, and hoping to smash the thing by a brutal bombardment of terrific voltage. We're trying, thanks to the results of those instruments, to get results with small, terrifically intense fields."

"How do you know that's their general system?"

"They left traces on the records of the post instruments. These records show such intensities as we never got. They have atomic energy, necessarily, and they might have had material energy, actual destruction of matter, but apparently, from the field readings it's the former. To be able to make those tremendous hops, light-years in length, they needed a real store of energy. They have accumulators, of course, but I don't think they could store enough power by the system they use to do it."

"Well, how's your trick 'bank' out on Luna, despite its twelve-foot walls, going to stand an atomic explosion?"

"More protective devices to come is our only hope. I'm working on three trails: atomic energy, some type of magnetic shield that will stop any moving material particle, and their faster-than-light thing. Also, that fortress—I mean, of course, bank—is going to have a lot of lead-lined rooms."

"I wish I could use the remaining money the Board gave me to lead-line a lot of those I.P. ships," said McLaurin wistfully. "Can't you make a gamma-ray bomb of some sort?"

"Not without their atomic energy release. With it, of course, it's easy to flood a region with rays. It'll be a million times worse than radium 'C,' which is bad enough."

"Well, I'll send through this petition for armaments. They'll pass it all right, I think. They may get some kicks from old Jacob Ezra Stubbs. Jacob Ezra doesn't believe in anything war-like. I wish they'd find some way to keep him off of the Arms Petition Board. He might just as well stay home and let 'em vote his ticket uniformly 'nay.'" Buck Kendall left with a laugh.

Buck Kendall had his troubles though. When he had reached Earth again, he found that his properties totaled one hundred and three million dollars, roughly. One doesn't sell properties of that magnitude, one borrows against them. But to all intents and purposes, Buck Kendall owned two half-completed ship's hulls in the Baldwin Spaceship Yards, a great deal of massive metal work on its way to Luna, and contracts for some very extensive work on a "bank." Beyond that, about eleven million was left.

A large portion of the money had been invested in a laboratory, the like of which the world had never seen. It was devoted exclusively to physics, and principally the physics of destruction. Dr. Paul Devin was the Director, Cole was in charge of the technical work, and Buck Kendall was free to do all the work he thought needed doing.

Returned to his laboratory, he looked sourly at the bench on which seven mechanicians were working. The ninth successive experiment on the release of atomic energy had failed. The tenth was in process of construction. A heavy pure tungsten dome, three feet in diameter, three inches thick, was being lowered over a clear insulum dome, a foot smaller. Inside, the real apparatus was arranged around the little pool of mercury. From it, two massive tungsten-copper alloy conductors led through the insulum housing, and outside. These, so Kendall had hoped, would surge with the power of broken atoms, but he was beginning to believe rather bitterly, they would never do so.

Buck went on to his offices, and the main calculator room. There were ten calculator tables here, two of them in operation now.

"Hello, Devin. Getting on?"

"No," said Devin bitterly, "I'm getting off. Look at these results." He brought over a sheaf of graphs, with explanatory tables attached. Rapidly Buck ran through them with him. Most of them were graphs of functions of light, considered as a wave in these experiments.

"H-m-m-m—not very encouraging. Looks like you've got the field—but it just snaps shut on itself and won't work. The lack of volume makes it break down, if you establish it, and makes it impossible to establish in the first place without the energy of matter. Not so hot. That's certainly cock-eyed somewhere."

"I'm not. The math may be."

"Well"—Kendall grinned—"it amounts to the same thing. The point is, light doesn't. Let's run over that theory again. Light is not only magnetic; but electric. Somehow it transforms electric fields cyclically into magnetic fields and back again. Now what we want to do is to transform an electric into a magnetic field and have it stay there. That's the first step. The second thing, is to have the lines of magnetic force you develop, lie down like a sheath around the ship, instead of standing out like the hairs on an angry cat, the way they want to. That means turning them ninety degrees, and turning an electric into a magnetic field means turning the space-strain ninety degrees. Light evidently forms a magnetic field whose lines of force reach along its direction of motion, so that's your starting point."

"Yes, and *that*," growled Devin, "seems to be the finishing point. Quite definitely and clearly, the graph looped down to zero. In other words, the field closed in on itself, and destroyed itself."

"Light doesn't vanish."

"I'll make you all the lights you want."

"I simply mean there must be something that will stop it."

"Certainly. Transform it back to electric field before it gets a chance to close in, then repeat the process—the way light does."

"That wouldn't make such a good magnetic shield. Every time that field started pulsing out through the walls of the ship it would generate heat. We want a permanent field that will stay on the job out there. I wonder if you couldn't make a conductor device that would open that field out—some special type of oscillating field that would keep it open."

"H-m-m-m—that's an angle I might try. Any suggestions?"

Kendall had suggestions, and rapidly he outlined a development that appeared from some of the earlier mathematics on light, and might be what they wanted.

Kendall, however, had problems of his own to work on. The question of atomic energy he was leaving alone, till the present experiment either succeeded, or, as he rather suspected, failed as had its predecessors. His present problem was to develop more fully some interesting lines of research he had run across in investigating mathematically the trick of turning electric to magnetic fields and then turning them back again. It might be that along this line he would find the answer to the speed greater than that of light. At any rate, he was interested.

He worked the rest of that day, and most of the next on that line—till he ran it into the ground with a pair of equations that ended with the expression: $dx.dv = h/(4\pi m)$. Then Kendall looked at them for a long moment, then he sighed gently and threw them into a file cabinet. Heisenberg's Uncertainty. He'd reduced the thing to a form that simply told him it was beyond the limits of certainty and he ran it into the normal, natural uncertainty inevitable in Nature.

Anyway he had real work to do now. The machine was about ready for his attention. The mechanicians had finished putting it in shape for demonstration and trial. He himself would have to test it over the rest of the afternoon and arrange for power and so forth.

By evening, when Commander McLaurin called around with some of the other investors in Kendall's "bank" on Luna, the thing was already started, warming up. The fields were being fed and the various scientists of the group were watching with interest. Power was flowing in already at a rate of nearly one hundred thousand horsepower per minute, thanks to a special line given them by New York Power (a Kendall property). At ten o'clock they were beginning to expect the reaction to start. By this time the fields weren't gaining in intensity very rapidly, a maximum intensity had been reached that should, they felt, break the atoms soon.

At eleven-thirty, through the little view window, Buck Kendall saw something that made him cry out in amazement. The mercury metal in the receiver, behind its layers of screening was beginning to glow, with a dull reddish light, and little solidifications were appearing in it!

Eagerly the men looked, as the solidifications spread slowly, like crystals growing in an evaporating solution.

Twelve o'clock came and went, and one o'clock and two o'clock. Still the slow crystallization went on. Buck Kendall was casting furtive glances at the kilowatt-hour meter. It stood at a figure that represented twenty-seven thousand dollars' worth of power. Long since the power rate had been increased to the maximum available, as the power plant's normal load reduced as the morning hours came. Surely, this time something would start, but Buck had two worries. If all the enormous amount of energy they had poured in there decided to release itself at once—

And at any rate, Buck saw they'd never dare to let a generator stop, once it was started!

The men were a tense group around the machine at three-fifteen A.M. There remained only a tiny, dancing globule of silvery mercury skittering around on the sharp, needle-like crystals of the dull red metal that had resulted. Slowly that skittering drop was shrinking…

Three twenty-two and a half A.M. saw the last fraction of it vanish. Tensely the men stared into the machine— backing off slowly—watching the meters on the board. At nearly eighty thousand volts the power had been fed into it.

The power continued to flow, and a growing halo of intense violet light appeared suddenly on those red, needle-like crystals, a swiftly expanding halo…

Without a sound, without the slightest disturbance, the halo vanished, and softly, gently, the needle-like crystals relapsed, melted away, and a dull pool of metallic mercury rested in the receiver.

At eighty thousand volts, power was flowing in…

And it didn't even sparkle.

CHAPTER FIVE

The apparatus of the magnetic shield had been completed two days later, and set up in Buck's own laboratory. On the bench was the powerful, but small, little projector of the straight magnetic field, simply a specially designed accumulator, a super-condenser, and the peculiar apparatus Devin had designed to distort the electric field through ninety degrees to a magnetic field. Behind this was a curious, paraboloid projector made up of hundreds of tiny, carefully orientated coils. This was Buck's own contribution. They were ready for the tests.

"I would invite McLaurin in to see this," said Kendall looking at them, and then across the room bitterly toward the alleged atomic power apparatus on the opposite bench. "I think it will work. But after *that*—" He stared, glaring, at the heavy tungsten dome with its heavy tungsten contacts, across which the flame of released atomic energy was supposed to have leapt. "That was probably the flattest flop any experiment ever flopped."

"Well—it didn't blow up. That's one comfort," suggested Devin.

"I wish it had. Then at least it would have shown some response. The only response shown, actually, was shown on the power meter. It damn near wore out the bearings turning so fast."

"Personally, I prefer the lack of action." Devin laughed. "Have you got that circuit hooked up?"

"Right," sighed Kendall, turning back to the work in hand. "Is Douglass in on this?"

"Yes—in the next room. He'll let us know when he's ready. He's setting up those instruments."

Douglass, a young junior physicist, late of the I.P. Physics Department, stuck his head in the door and announced his instruments were all set up.

"Keep an eye on them. They'll move somehow, at any rate. This thing couldn't go as flat as that atom-buster of mine."

Carefully Kendall made a few last-minute adjustments on the limiting relays, and took up his position at the power board. Devin took his place near the apparatus, with another series of instruments, similar to those Douglass was now watching in the next room, some thirty feet away, through the two-inch metal wall. "Ready," called Kendall.

The switch shot home. Instantly Kendall, Devin, and all the men in the building jumped some six feet from their former positions. A monstrous roar of sound crashed out in that laboratory that thundered from one wall to the other, and bellowed in a Titan's fury. It thundered and growled, it bellowed and howled, the walls shook with the march and counter-march of crashing waves of sound.

And a ten-foot wavering flame of blue-white, bellying electric fire shuddered up to the ceiling from the contact points of the alleged atomic generator. The heat, pouring out from the flashing, roaring arc sent prickles of aching burns over Kendall's skin. For ten seconds he stood in utter, paralyzed surprise as his flop of flops bellowed its anger at his disdain. Then he leapt to the power board and shut off the roaring thing, by cutting the switch that had started it.

"Spirits of Space! Did *that* come to life!"

"*Atomic Energy!*" Devin cried.

"Atomic energy, hell. That's my thirty thousand dollars' worth of power breaking loose again," chortled Kendall.

"We missed the atomic energy, but, sweet boy, what an accumulator we stubbed our toes on! I wondered where in blazes all that power went to. That's the answer. I'll bet I can tell you right now what happened. We built that mercury up to a new level, and that transitional stage was the red, crystalline metal. When it reached the higher stage, it was temporarily stable—but that projector over there that we designed for the purpose of holding open electric and magnetic fields just opened the door and let all that power right out again."

"But why isn't it atomic energy? How do you know that no more than your power that you put in is coming out?" demanded Devin.

"The arc, man, the arc. That was a high-current, and low-voltage arc. Couldn't you tell by the sound that no great voltage—as atomic voltages go—was smashing across there? If we were getting atomic voltage—and power—there'd have been a different tone to it, high and shriller.

"Now, did you take any readings?"

"What do you think, man? I'm human. Do you think I got any readings with that thing bellowing and shrieking in my ears, and burning my skin with ultra-violet? It itches now."

Kendall laughed. "You know what to do for an itch. Now, I'm going to make a bet. We had those points separated for a half-million volts discharge, but there was a dust-cover thrown over them just now. That, you notice, is missing. I'll bet that served as a starter lead for the main arc. Now I'm going to start that projector thing again, and move the points there through about six inches, and that thing probably won't start itself."

Most of the laboratory staff had collected at the doorway, looking in at the white-hot tungsten discharge points, and the now silent "atomic engine." Kendall turned to them and said: "The flop picked itself up. You go on back, we seem to be all in one piece yet. Douglass, you didn't get any readings, did you?"

Sheepishly, Douglass grinned at him. "Eh—er—no—but I tore my pants. The magnetic field grabbed me and I jumped. They had some steel buttons, and a lot of steel keys—they're kinda' hard to keep on now."

The laboratory staff broke into a roar of laughter, as Douglass, holding up his trousers with both hands was beheld.

"I guess the field worked," he said.

"I guess maybe it did," adjudged Kendall solemnly. "We have some rope here if you need it—"

Douglass returned to his post.

Swiftly, Kendall altered the atomic distortion storage apparatus, and returned to the power-board. "Ready?"

"Check."

Kendall shoved home the switch. The storage device was silent. Only a slight feeling of strain made itself felt, and the sudden noisy hum of a small transformer nearby. "She works, Buck!" Devin called. "The readings check almost exactly."

"All good then. Now I want to get to that atomic thing. We can let that slide for a little bit—I'll answer it."

The telephone had rung noisily. "Kendall Labs—Kendall speaking."

"This is Superintendent Foster, of the New York Power, Mr. Kendall. We have some trouble just now that we think your operations may be responsible for. The sub-station at North Beaumont blew all the fuses, and threw the breakers at the main station. The men out there said the transformers began howling—"

"Right you are—I'm afraid I did do that. I had no idea that it would reach so far. How far is that from my place here?"

"It's about a thousand yards, according to the survey maps."

"Thanks—and I'll be careful about it. Any damage, I am responsible for? All okay?"

"Yes, sir, Mr. Kendall."

Kendall hung up. "We stirred up a lot more dust than we expected, Devin. Now let's start seeing if we can keep track of it. Douglass, how did your readings show?"

"I took them at the ten stations, and here they are. The stations are two feet apart."

"H-m-m—.5—.55—.6—.7—20—198—5950—6010—6012—5920. Very, very nice—only the darned thing's got an arm as long as the law. Your readings were about .2, Devin?"

"That's right."

"Then these little readings are just leakage. What's our normal intensity here?"

"About .19. Just a very small fraction less than the readings."

"Perfect—we have what amounts to a hollow shell of magnetic force—we can move inside, and you can move outside—far enough. But you can't get a conductor or a magnetic field through it." He put the readings on the bench, and looked at the apparatus across the room. "Now I want to start right on that other. Douglass, you move that magnetostat apparatus out of the way, and leave just the 'can-opener' of ours—the projector. I'm pretty sure that's what does the deed. Devin, see if you can hunt up some electrostatic voltmeters with a range in the neighborhood of—I think it'll be about eighty thousand."

Rapidly, Douglass was dismounting the apparatus, as Devin started for the stock room. Kendall started making some new connections, reconnecting the apparatus they had intended using on the "atomic engine," largely high-capacity resistances. He seemed to perform this work mechanically, his mind definitely on something else. Suddenly he stopped, and looked carefully into the receiver of the machine. The metal in it was silvery, liquid, and here and there a floating crystal of the dull red metal. Slowly a smile spread across his face. He turned to Douglass.

"Douglass—ah, you're through. Get on the trail of MacBride, and get him and his crew to work making half a dozen smaller things like this. Tell 'em they can leave off the tungsten shield. I want different metals in the receiver of each. Use—hmmm—sodium—copper—magnesium—aluminium, iron and chromium. Got it?"

"Yes, sir." He left, just as Devin returned with a large electrostatic voltmeter.

"I'd like," said he, "to know how you know the voltage will range around eighty thousand."

"K-ring excitation potential for mercury. I'm willing to bet that thing simply shoved the whole electron system of the mercury out a notch—that it simply *hasn't* any K-ring of electrons now. I'm trying some other metals. Douglass is going to have MacBride make up half a dozen more machines. Machines—they need a name. This—ah—this is an 'atostor.' MacBride's going to make up half a dozen of 'em, and try half a dozen metals. I'm almost certain that's not mercury in there now, at all. It's probably element 99 or something like it."

"It looks like mercury—"

"Certainly. So would 99. Following the periodic table, 99 would probably have an even lower melting point than mercury, be silvery, dense and heavy—and perhaps slightly radioactive. The series under the B family of Group II is Magnesium, Zinc, Cadmium, Mercury—and 99. The melting point is going down all the way, and they're all silvery metals. I'm going to try copper, and I fully expect it to turn silvery—in fact, to become silver."

"Then let's see." Swiftly they hooked up the apparatus, realigned the projector, and again Kendall took his place at the power-board. As he closed the switch, on no-load, the electrostatic voltmeter flopped over instantly, and steadied at just over 80,000 volts.

"I hate to say 'I told you so,'" said Kendall. "But let's hook in a load. Try it on about 100 amps first."

Devin began cutting in load. The resistors began heating up swiftly as more and more current flowed through them. By not so much as by a vibration of the voltmeter needle, did the apparatus betray any strain as the load mounted swiftly. 100—200—500—1000 amperes. Still, that needle held steady. Finally, with a drain of ten thousand amperes, all the equipment available could handle, the needle was steady as a rock, though the tremendous load of 800,000,000 watts was cut in and out. That, to atoms, atoms by the nonillions, was no appreciable load at all. There was *no* internal resistance whatever. The perfect accumulator had certainly been discovered.

"I'll have to call McLaurin—" Kendall hurried away with a broad, broad smile.

CHAPTER SIX

"Hello, Tom?"

The telephone rattled in a peeved sort of way. "Yes, it is. What now? And when am I going to see you in a social sort of way again?"

"Not for a long, long time; I'm busy. I'm busy right now as a matter of fact. I'm calling up the vice-president of Faragaut Interplanetary Lines, and I want to place an order."

"Why bother me? We have clerks, you know, for that sort of thing," suggested Faragaut in a pained voice.

"Tom, do you know how much I'm worth now?"

"Not much," replied Faragaut promptly. "What of it? I hear, as a matter of fact that you're worth even less in a business way. They're talking quite a lot down this way about an alleged bank you're setting up on Luna. I hear it's got more protective devices, and armor than any I.P. station in the System, that you even had it designed by an I.P. designer, and have a gang of Colonels and Generals in charge. I also hear that you've succeeded in getting rid of money at about one million dollars a day—just slightly shy of that."

"You overestimate me, my friend. Much of that is merely contracted for. Actually it'll take me nearly nine months to get rid of it. And by that time I'll have more. Anyway, I think I have something like ten million left. And remember that way back in the twentieth century some old fellow beat my record. Armour, I think it was, lost a million dollars a day for a couple of months running.

"Anyway, what I called you up for was to say I'd like to order five hundred thousand tons of mercury, for delivery as soon as possible."

"What! Oh, say, I thought you were going in for business." Faragaut gave a slight laugh of relief.

"Tom, I am. I mean exactly what I say. I want five—hundred—thousand—*tons* of metallic mercury, and just as soon as you can get it."

"Man, there isn't that much in the system."

"I know it. Get all there is on the market for me, and contract to take all the 'Jupiter Heavy-Metals' can turn out. You send those orders through, and clean out the market completely. Somebody's about to pay for the work I've been doing, and boy, they're going to pay through the nose. After you've got that order launched, and don't make a christening party of the launching either, why just drop out here, and I'll show you why the value of mercury is going so high you won't be able to follow it in a space ship."

"The cost of that," said Faragaut, seriously now, "will be about—fifty-three million at the market price. You'd have to put up twenty-six cash, and I don't believe you've got it."

Buck laughed. "Tom, loan me a dozen million, will you? You send that order through, and then come see what I've got. I've got a break, too! Mercury's the best metal for this use—and it'll stop gamma rays too!"

"So it will—but for the love of the system, what of it?"

"Come and see—tonight. Will you send that order through?"

"I will, Buck. I hope you're right. Cash is tight now, and I'll probably have to put up nearer twenty million, when all that buying goes through. How long will it be tied up in that deal, do you think?"

"Not over three weeks. And I'll guarantee you three hundred percent—if you'll stay in with me after you start.

Otherwise—I don't think making this money would be fair just now."

"I'll be out to see you in about two hours, Buck. Where are you? At the estate?" asked Faragaut seriously.

"In my lab out there. Thanks, Tom."

McLaurin was there when Tom Faragaut arrived. And General Logan, and Colonel Gerardhi. There was a restrained air of gratefulness about all of them that Tom Faragaut couldn't quite understand. He had been looking up Buck Kendall's famous bank, and more and more he had begun to wonder just what was up. The list of stockholders had read like a list of I.P. heroes and executives. The staff had been a list of I.P. men with a slender sprinkling of accountants. And the sixty-million dollar structure was to be a bank without advertising of any sort! Usually such a venture is planned and published months in advance. This had sprung up suddenly, with a strange quietness.

Almost silently, Buck Kendall led the way to the laboratory. A small metal tank was supported in a peculiar piece of apparatus, and from it led a small platinum pipe to a domed apparatus made largely of insulum. A little pool of mercury, with small red crystals floating in it rested in a shallow hollow surrounded by heavy conductors.

"That's it, Tom. I wanted to show you first what we have, and why I wanted all that mercury. Within three weeks, every man, woman and child in the system will be clamoring for mercury metal. That's the perfect accumulator." Quickly he demonstrated the machine, charging it, and then discharging it. It was better than 99.95% efficient on the charge, and was 100% efficient on the discharge.

"Physically, any metal will do. Technically, mercury is best for a number of reasons. It's a liquid. I can, and do it in this, charge a certain quantity, and then move it up to the storage tank. Charge another pool, and move it up. In discharge, I can let a stream flow in continuously if I required a steady, terrific drain of power without interruption. If I wanted it for more normal service, I'd discharge a pool, drain it, refill the receiver, and discharge a second pool. Thus, mercury is the metal to use.

"Do you see why I wanted all that metal?"

"I do, Buck—Lord, I do," gasped Faragaut. "That is the perfect power supply."

"No, confound it, it isn't. It's a secondary source. It isn't primary. We're just as limited in the *supply* of power as ever—only we have increased our distribution of power. Lord knows, we're going to need a power *supply* badly enough before long—" Buck relapsed into moody silence.

"What," asked Faragaut, looking around him, "does that mean?"

It was McLaurin who told him of the stranger ship, and Kendall's interpretation of its meaning. Slowly Faragaut grasped the meaning behind Buck's strange actions of the past months.

"The Lunar Bank," he said slowly, half to himself. "Staffed by trained I.P. men, experts in expert destruction. Buck, you said something about the profits of this venture. What did you mean?"

Buck smiled. "We're going to stick up I.P. to the extent necessary to pay for that fort—er—bank—on Luna. We'll also boost the price so that we'll make enough to pay for those ships I'm having made. The public will pay for that."

"I see. And we aren't to stick the price too high, and just make money?"

"That's the general idea."

"The I.P. Appropriations Board won't give you what you need, Commander, for real improvements on the I.P. ships?"

"They won't believe Kendall. Therefore they won't."

"What did you mean about gamma rays, Buck?"

"Mercury will stop them and the Commander here intends to have the refitted ships built so that the engine room and control room are one, and completely surrounded by the mercury tanks. The men will be protected against the gamma rays."

"Won't the rays affect the power stored in the mercury—perhaps release it?"

"We tried it out, of course, and while we can't get the intensities we expect, and can't really make any measurements of the gamma-ray energy impinging on the mercury—it seems to absorb, and store that energy!"

"What's next on the program, Buck?"

"Finish those ships I have building. And I want to do some more development work. The Stranger will return within six months now, I believe. It will take all that time, and more for real refitting of the I.P. ships."

"How about more forts—or banks, whichever you want to call them. Mars isn't protected."

"Mars is abandoned," replied General Logan seriously. "We haven't any too much to protect old Earth, and she must come first. Mars will, of course, be protected as best the I.P. ships can. But—we're expecting defeat. This isn't a case of glorious victory. It will be a case of hard won survival. We don't know anything about the enemy—except that they are capable of interstellar flights, and have atomic energy. They are evidently far ahead of us. Our battle is to survive till we learn how to conquer. For a time, at least, the Strangers will have possession of most of the planets of the system. We do not think they will be able to reach Earth, because Commander McLaurin here will withdraw his ships to Earth to protect the planet—and the great 'Lunar Bank' will display its true character."

CHAPTER SEVEN

Faragaut looked unsympathetically at Buck Kendall, as he stood glaring perplexedly at the apparatus he had been working on.

"What's the matter, Buck, won't she perk?"

"No, damn it, and it should."

"That," pointed out Faragaut, "is just what you think. Nature thinks otherwise. We generally have to abide by her opinions. What is it—or what is it meant to be?"

"Perfect reflector."

"Make a nice mirror. What else, and how come?"

"A mirror is just what I want. I want something that will reflect *all* the radiation that falls on it. No metal will, even in its range of maximum reflectivity. Aluminum goes pretty high, silver, on some ranges, a bit higher. But none of them reaches 99%. I want a perfect reflector that I can put behind a source of wild, radiant energy so I can focus it, and put it where it will do the most good."

"Ninety-nine percent. Sounds pretty good. That's better efficiency than most anything else we have, isn't it?"

"No, it isn't. The accumulator is 100% efficient on the discharge, and a good transformer, even before that, ran as high as 99.8 sometimes. They had to. If you have a transformer handling 1,000,000 horsepower, and it's even 1% inefficient, you have a heat loss of nearly 10,000 horsepower to handle. I want to use this as a destructive weapon, and if I hand the other fellow energy in distressing amounts, it's even worse at my end, because no matter how perfect a beam I work out, there will still be some spread. I can make it mighty tight though, if I make my surface a perfect parabola. But if I send a million horse, I have to handle it, and a ship can't stand several hundred thousand horsepower roaming around loose as heat, let alone the weapon itself. The thing will be worse to me than to him.

"I figured there was something worth investigating in those fields we developed on our magnetic shield work. They had to do, you know, with light, and radiant energy. There must be some reason why a metal reflects. Further, though we can't get down to the basic root of matter, the atom, yet, we can play around just about as we please with molecules and molecular forces. But it is molecular force that determines whether light and radiant energy of that caliber shall be reflected or transmitted. Take aluminum as an example. In the metallic molecule state, the metal will reflect pretty well. But volatilize it, and it becomes transparent. All gases are transparent, all metals reflective. Then the secret of perfect reflection lies at a molecular level in the organization of matter, and is within our reach. Well—this thing was supposed to make that piece of silver reflective. I missed it that time." He sighed. "I suppose I'll have to try again."

"I should think you'd use tungsten for that. If you do have a slight leak, that would handle the heat."

"No, it would hold it. Silver is a better conductor of heat. But the darned thing won't work."

"Your other scheme has." Faragaut laughed. "I came out principally for some signatures. I.P. wants one hundred thousand tons of mercury. I've sold most of mine already in the open market. You want to sell?"

"Certainly. And I told you my price."

"I know," sighed Faragaut. "It seems a shame though. Those I.P. board men would pay higher. And they're so damn tight it seems a crime not to make 'em pay up when they have to."

"The I.P. will need the money worse elsewhere. Where do I—oh, here?"

"Right. I'll be out again this evening. The regular group will be here?"

Kendall nodded as he signed in triplicate.

That evening, Buck had found the trouble in his apparatus, for as he well knew, the theory was right, only the practical apparatus needed changing. Before the group composed of Faragaut, McLaurin and the members of Kendall's "bank," he demonstrated it.

It was merely a small, model apparatus, with a mirror of space-strained silver that was an absolutely perfect reflector. The mirror had been ground out of a block of silver one foot deep, by four inches square, carefully annealed, and the work had all been done in a cooling bath. The result was a mirror that was so nearly a perfect paraboloid that the beam held sharp and absolutely tight for the half-mile range they tested it on. At the projector it was three and one-half inches in diameter. At the target, it was three and fifty-two one hundredths inches in diameter.

"Well, you've got the mirror, what are you going to reflect with it now?" asked McLaurin. "The greatest problem is getting a radiant source, isn't it? You can't get a temperature above about ten thousand degrees, and maintain it very long, can you?"

"Why not?" Kendall smiled.

"It'll volatilize and leave the scene of action, won't it?"

"What if it's a gaseous source already?"

"What? Just a gas-flame? That won't give you the point source you need. You're using just a spotlight here, with a Moregan Point-light. That won't give you energy, and if you use a gas-flame, the spread will be so great, that no matter how perfectly you figure your mirror, it won't beam."

"The answer is easy. Not an ordinary gas-flame—a very extra-special kind of gas-flame. Know anything about Renwright's ionization-work?"

"Renwright—he's an I.P. man isn't he?"

"Right. He's developed a system, which, thanks to the power we can get in that atostor, will sextuply ionize oxygen gas. Now: what does that mean?"

"Spirits of space! Concentrated essence of energy!"

"Right. And in preparation, Cole here had one made up for me. That—and something else. We'll just hook it up—"

With Devin's aid, Kendall attached the second apparatus, a larger device into which the silver block with its mirror surface fitted. With the uttermost care, the two physicists lined it up. Two projectors pointed toward each other at an angle, the base angles of a triangle, whose apex was the center of the mirror. On very low power, a soft, glowing violet light filtered out through the opening of the one, and a slight green light came from the other. But where the two streams met, an intense, violet glare built up. The center of action was not at the focus, and slowly this was lined up, till a sharp, violet beam of light reached out across the open yard to the target set up.

Buck Kendall cut off the power, and slowly got into position. "Now. Keep out from in front of that thing. Put on these glasses—and watch out." Heavy, thick-lensed orange-brown goggles were passed out, and Kendall took his place. Before him, a thick window of the same glass had been arranged, so that he might see uninterruptedly the controls at hand, and yet watch unblinded, the action of the beam.

Dully the mirror-force relay clicked. A hazy glow ran over the silver block, and died. Then—simultaneously the power was thrown from two small, compact atostors into the twin projectors. Instantly—a titanic eruption of light almost invisibly violet, spurted out in a solid, compact stream. With a roar and crash, it battered its way through the thick air, and crashed into the heavy target plate. A stream of flame and scintillating sparks erupted from the armor plate—and died as Kendall cut the beam. A white-hot area a foot across leaked down the face of the metal.

"That," said Faragaut gently, removing his goggles. "That's not a spotlight, and it's not exactly a gas-flame. But I still don't know what that blue-hot needle of destruction is. Just what do you call that tame stellar furnace of yours?"

"Not so far off, Tom," said Kendall happily, "except that even S Doradus is cold compared to that. That sends almost pure ultra-violet light—which, by the way, it is almost impossible to reflect successfully, and represents a temperature to be expressed not in thousands of degrees, nor yet in tens of thousands. I calculated the temperature would be about 750,000 degrees. What is happening is that a stream of low-voltage electrons—cathode rays—in great quantity are meeting great quantities of sextuply ionized oxygen. That means that a nucleus used to having two electrons in the K-ring, and six in the next, has had that outer six knocked off, and then has been hurled violently into free air.

"All by themselves, those sextuply ionized oxygen atoms would have a good bit to say, but they don't really begin to talk till they start roaring for those electrons I'm feeding them. At the meeting point, they grab up all they can get—probably about five—before the competition and the fierce release of energy drives them out, part-satisfied. I lose a little energy there, but not a real fraction. It's the howl they put up for the first four that counts. The electron-feed is necessary, because otherwise they'd smash on and ruin that mirror. They work practically in a perfect vacuum. That beam smashes the air out of the way. Of course, in space it would work better."

"How could it?" asked Faragaut, faintly.

"Kendall," asked McLaurin, "can we install that in the I.P. ships?"

"You can start." Kendall shrugged. "There isn't a lot of apparatus. I'm going to install them in my ships, and in the—bank. I suspect—we haven't a lot of time left."

"How near ready are those ships?"

"About. That's all I can say. They've been torn up a bit for installation of the atostor apparatus. Now they'll have to be changed again."

"Anything more coming?"

Buck smiled slowly. He turned directly to McLaurin and replied: "Yes—the Strangers. As to developments—I can't tell, naturally. But if they do, it will be something entirely unexpected now. You see, given one new discovery, a half-dozen will follow immediately from it. When we announced that atostor, look what happened. Renwright must have thought it was God's gift to suffering physicists. He stuck some oxygen in the thing, added some of his own stuff—and behold. The magnetic apparatus gave us directly the shield, and indirectly this mirror. Now,

I seem to have reached the end for the time. I'm still trying to get that space-release for high speed—speed greater than light, that is. So far," he added bitterly, "all I've gotten as an answer is a single expression that simply means practical zero—Heisenberg's Uncertainty Expression."

"I'm uncertain as to your meaning…" McLaurin smiled. "…but I take it that's nothing new."

"No. Nearly four centuries old—twentieth century physics. I'll have to try some other line of attack, I guess, but that did seem so darned right. It just sounded right. Something ought to happen—and it just keeps saying 'nothing more except the natural uncertainty of nature.'"

"Try it out, your math might be wrong somewhere."

Kendall laughed. "If it was—I'd hate to try it out. If it wasn't I'd have no reason to. And there's plenty of other work to do. For one thing, getting that apparatus in production. The I.P. board won't like me." Kendall smiled.

"They don't," replied McLaurin. "They're getting more and more and more worried—but they've got to keep the I.P. fleet in such condition that it can at least catch an up-to-date freighter."

Gresth Gkae looked back at Sthor rapidly dropping behind, and across at her sister world, Asthor, circling a bare 100,000 miles away. Behind his great interstellar cruiser came a long line of similar ships. Each was loaded now not with instruments and pure scientists, but with weapons, fuel and warriors. Colonists too, came in the last ships. One hundred and fifty giant ships. All the wealth of Sthor and Asthor had been concentrated in producing those great machines. Every one represented nearly the equivalent of thirty million Earth-dollars. Four and a half billions of dollars for mere materials.

Gresth Gkae had the honor of lead position, for he had discovered the planets and their stable, though tiny, sun. Still, Gresth Gkae knew his own giant Mira was a super-giant sun—and a curse and a menace to any rational society. Our yellow-white sun (to his eyes, an almost invisible color, similar to our blue) was small, but stable, and warm enough.

In half an hour, all the ships were in space, and at a given signal, at ten-second intervals, they sprang into the superspeed, faster than light. For an instant, giant Mira ran and seemed distorted, as though seen through a porthole covered with running water, then steadied, curiously distorted. Faster than light they raced across the galaxy.

Even in their super-fast ships, nearly three and a half weeks passed before the sun they sought, singled itself from the star-field as an extra bright point. Two days more, and the sun was within planetary distance. They came at an angle to the plane of the ecliptic, but they leveled down to it now, and slanted toward giant Jupiter and Jovian worlds. Ten worlds, in one sweep, it was—four habitable worlds. The nine satellites would be converted into forts at once, nine space-sweeping forts guarding the approaches to the planet. Gresth Gkae had made a fairly good search of the worlds, and knew that Earth was the main home of civilization in this system. Mars was second, and Venus third. But Jupiter offered the greatest possibilities for quick settlement, a base from which they could more easily operate, a base for fuels, for the heavy elements they would need...

Fifteen million miles from Jupiter they slowed below the speed of light—and the I.P. stations observed them.

Instantly, according to instructions issued by Commander McLaurin, a fleet of ten of the tiniest, fastest scouts darted out. As soon as possible, a group of three heavy cruisers, armed with all the inventions that had been discovered, the atostor power system, perfectly conducting power leads, the terrible UV ray, started out.

The scouts got there first. Cameras were grinding steadily, with long range telescopic lenses, delicate instruments probed and felt and caught their fingers in the fields of the giant fleet.

At ten-second intervals, giant ships popped into being, and glided smoothly toward Jupiter.

Then the cruisers arrived. They halted at a respectful distance, and waited. The Miran ships plowed on undisturbed. Simultaneously, from the three leaders, terrific neutron rays shot out. The paraffin block walls stopped those—and the cruisers started to explain their feelings on the subject. They were the IP-J-37, 39, and 42. The 37 turned up the full power of the UV ray. The terrific beam of ultra-violet energy struck the second Miran ship, and the spot it touched exploded into incandescence, burned white-hot—and puffed out abruptly as the air pressure within blew the molten metal away.

The Mirans were startled. This was not the type of thing Gresth Gkae had warned them of. Gresth Gkae himself frowned as the sudden roar of the machines of his ship rose in the metal walls. A stream of ten-inch atomic bombs shrieked out of their tubes, fully glowing green things floated out more slowly, and immediately waxed brilliant. Gamma ray bombs—but they could be guarded against—

The three Solarian cruisers were washed in such frightful flame as they had never imagined. Streams of atomic bombs were exploding soundlessly, ineffectively in space, not thirty feet from them as they felt the sudden resistance of the magnetic shields. Hopefully, the 39 probed with her neutron gun. Nothing happened save that several gamma ray bombs went off explosively, and all the atomic bombs in its path exploded at once.

Gresth Gkae knew what that meant. Neutron beam guns. Then this race was more intelligent than he had believed. They had not had them before. Had he perhaps given them too much warning and information?

There was a sudden, deeper note in the thrumming roar of the great ship. Eagerly Gresth Gkae watched—and sighed in relief. The nearer of the three enemy ships was crumbling to dust. Now the other two were beginning to become blurred of outline. They were fleeing—but oh, so slowly. Easily the greater ship chased them down, till only floating dust, and a few small pieces of...

Gresth Gkae shrieked in pain, and horror. The destroyed ships had fought in dying. All space seemed to blossom out with a terrible light, a light that wrapped around them, and burned into him, and through him. His eyes were dark and burning lumps in his head, his flesh seemed crawling, stinging—he was being flayed alive—in shrieking agony he crumpled to the floor.

Hospital attachés came to him, and injected drugs. Slowly torturing consciousness left him. The doctors began working over his horribly burned body, shuddering inwardly as the protective, feather-like covering of his skin loosened, and dropped from his body. Tenderly they lowered him into a bath of chemicals...

"The terrible light which caused so much damage to our men," reported a physicist, "was analyzed, and found to have some extraordinary lines. It was largely mercury-vapor spectrum, but the spectrum of mercury-atoms in an impossibly strained condition. I would suggest that great care be used hereafter, and all men be equipped with protective masks when observations are needed. This sun is very rich in the infra-X-rays and ultra-visible light. The explosion of light, we witnessed, was dangerous in its consisting almost wholly of very short and hard infra-X-rays."

The physicist had a special term for what we know as ultra-violet light. To him, blue was ultra-violet, and exceedingly dangerous to red-sensitive eyes. To him, our ultra-violet was a long X-ray, and was designated by a special term. And to him—the explosion of the atostor reservoirs was a terrible and mystifying calamity.

To the men in the five tiny scout-ships, it was also a surprise, and a painful one. Even space-hardened humans were burned by the terrifically hard ultra-violet from the explosion. But they got some hint of what it had meant to the Mirans from the confusion that resulted in the fleet. Several of the nearer ships spun, twisted, and went erratically off their courses. All seemed uncontrolled momentarily.

The five scouts, following orders, darted instantly toward the Lunar Bank. Why, they did not know. But those were orders. They were to land there.

The reason was that, faster than any Solarian ship, radio signals had reached McLaurin, and he, and most of the staff of the I.P. service had been moved to the Lunar Bank. Buck Kendall had extended an invitation in this "unexpected emergency." It so happened that Buck Kendall's invitation got there before any description of the Strangers, or their actions had arrived. The staff was somewhat puzzled as to how this happened...

And now for the satellites of great Jupiter.

One hundred and fifty giant interstellar cruisers advanced on Callisto. They didn't pause to investigate the mines and scattered farms of the satellite, but ten great ships settled, and a horde of warriors began pouring out.

One hundred and forty ships reached Ganymede. One hundred and thirty sailed on. One hundred and thirty ships reached Europa—and they sailed on hurriedly, one hundred and twenty-nine of them. Gresth Gkae did not know it then, but the fleet had lost its first ship. The I.P. station on Europa had spoken back.

They sailed in, a mighty armada, and the first dropped through Europa's thin, frozen atmosphere. They spotted the dome of the station, and a neutron ray lashed out at it. On the other, undefended worlds, this had been effective. Here—it was answered by ten five-foot UV rays. Further, these men had learned something from the destruction of the cruisers, and ten torpedoes had been unloaded, reloaded with atostor mercury, and sent out bravely.

Easily the Mirans wiped out the first torpedo...

Shrieking, the Miran pilots clawed their way from the controls as the fearful flood of ultra-violet light struck their unaccustomed skins. Others too felt that burning flood.

The second torpedo they caught and deflected on a beam of alternating-current magnetism that repelled it. It did not come nearer than half a mile to the ship. The third they turned their deflecting beam on—and something went strangely wrong with the beam. It pulled that torpedo toward the ship with a sickening acceleration—and the torpedo exploded in that frightful violet flame.

Five-foot diameter UV beams are nothing to play with. The Mirans were dodging these now as they loosed atomic bombs, only to see them exploded harmlessly by neutron guns, or caught in the magnetic screen. Gamma ray bombs were as useless. Again the beam of disintegrating force was turned on...

The present opponent was not a ship. It was an I.P. defense station, equipped with everything Solarian science knew, and the dome was an eight-foot wall of tungsten-beryllium. The eight feet of solid, ultra-resistant alloy drank up that crumbling beam, and liked it. The wall did not fail. The men inside the fort jerked and quivered as the strange beam, a small, small fraction of it, penetrated the eight feet of outer wall, the six feet or so of intervening walls, and the mercury atostor reserves.

"Concentrate all those UV beams on one spot, and see if you can blast a hole in him before he shakes it loose," ordered the ray technician. "He'll wiggle if you start off with the beam. Train your sights on the nose of that first ship—when you're ready, call out."

"Ready—ready—" Ten men replied. "Fire!" roared the technician. Ten titanic swords of pure ultra-violet energy, energy that practically no unconditioned metal will reflect to more than fifty per cent, emerged. There was a single spot of intense incandescence for a single hundredth of a second—and then the energy was burning its way through the inner, thinner skins with such rapidity that they sputtered and flickered like a broken televisor.

One hundred and twenty-nine ships retreated hastily for conference, leaving a gutted, wrecked hull, broken by its fall, on Europa. Triumphantly, the Europa I.P. station hurled out its radio message of the first encounter between a fort and the Miran forces.

Most important of all, it sent a great deal of badly wanted information regarding the Miran weapons.

Particularly interesting was the fact that it had withstood the impact of that disintegrating ray.

CHAPTER EIGHT

Grimly Buck Kendall looked at the reports. McLaurin stood beside him, Devin sat across the table from him. "What do you make of it, Buck?" asked the Commander.

"That we have just one island of resistance left on the Jovian worlds. And that will, I fear, vanish. They haven't finished with their arsenal by any means."

"But what was it, man, what was it that ruined those ships?"

"Vibration. Somehow—Lord only knows how it's done—they can project electric fields. These projected fields are oscillated, and they are tuned in with some parts of the ship. I suspect they are crystals of the metals. If they can start a vibration in the crystals of the metal—that's fatigue, metal fatigue enormously speeded. You know how a quartz crystal oscillator in a radio-control apparatus will break, if you work it on a very heavy load at the peak? They simply smash the crystals of metal in the same way. Only they project their field."

"Then our toughest metals are useless? Can't something tough, rather than hard, like copper or even silver for instance, stand it?"

"Calcium metal's the toughest going—and even that would break under the beating those ships give it. The only way to withstand it is to have such a mass of metal that the oscillations are damped out. But—"

The set tuned in on the I.P. station on Europa was speaking again. "The ships are returning. There are one hundred and twenty-nine by accurate count. Jorgsen reports that telescopic observation of the dead on the fallen cruiser show them to be a *completely un-human race*! They are of mottled coloring, predominately grayish brown. The ships are returning. They have divided into ten groups, nine groups of two each, and a main body of the rest of the fleet. The group of eighteen is descending within range, and we are focusing our beams on them—"

Out by Europa, ten great UV beams were stabbing angrily toward ten great interstellar ships. The metal of the hulls glowed brilliant, and distorted slowly as the thick walls softened under the heat, and the air behind pressed against it. Grimly the ten ships came on. Torpedoes were being launched, and exploded, and now they had no effect, for the Mirans within were protected.

The eighteen grouped ships separated, and arranged themselves in a circle around the fort. Suddenly one staggered as a great puff of gas shot out through the thin atmosphere of Europa to flare brilliantly in the lash of the stabbing UV beam. Instantly the ship righted itself, and labored upward. Another dropped to take its place...

And the great walls of the I.P. fort suddenly groaned and started in their welded joints. The faint, whispering rustle of the crumbling beam was murmuring through the station. Engineers shouted suddenly as meters leapt the length of their scales, and the needles clicked softly on the stop pins. A thin rustle came from the atostors grouped in the great power room. "Spirits of Space—a revolving magnetic field!" roared the Chief Technician. "They're making this whole blasted station a squirrel cage!"

The mighty walls of eight-foot metal shuddered and trembled. The UV beams lashed out from the fort in quivering arcs now, they did not hold their aim steady, and the magnetic shield that protected them from atomic bombs was working and straining wildly. Eighteen great ships quivered and tugged outside there now, straining with all their power to remain in the same spot, as they passed on from one to another the magnetic impulses that were now creating a titanic magnetic vortex about the fort.

"The atostors will be exhausted in another fifteen minutes," the Chief Technician roared into his transmitter. "Can the signals get through those fields, Commander?"

"No, Mac. They've been stopped, Sparks tells me. We're here—and let's hope we stay. What's happening?"

"They've got a revolving magnetic field out there that would spin a minor planet. The whole blasted fort is acting like the squirrel cage in an induction motor! They've made us the armature in a five hundred million horsepower electric motor."

"They can't tear this place loose, can they?"

"I don't know—it was never—" The Chief stopped. Outside a terrific roar and crash had built up. White darts of flame leapt a thousand feet into the air, hurling terrific masses of shattered rock and soil.

"I was going to say," the Chief went on, "this place wasn't designed for that sort of a strain. Our own magnetic field is supporting us now, preventing their magnetic field from getting its teeth on metal. When the strain comes—well, they're cutting loose our foundation with atomic bombs!"

Five UV beams were combined on one interstellar ship. Instantly the great machine retreated, and another dropped in to take its place while the magnetic field spun on, uninterruptedly.

"Can they keep that up long?"

"God knows—but they have a hundred and more ships to send in when the power of one gives out, remember."

"What's our reserve now?"

The Chief paused a moment to look at the meters. "Half what it was ten minutes ago!"

Commander Wallace sent some other orders. Every torpedo tube of the station suddenly belched forth deadly, fifteen-foot torpedoes, most of them mud-torpedoes, torpedoes loaded with high explosive in the nose, a delayed fuse, and a load of soft clinging mud in the rear. The mud would flow down over the nose and offer a resistance foothold for the explosive which empty space would not. Four hundred and three torpedoes, equipped with anti-magnetic apparatus darted out. One hundred and four passed the struggling fields. One found lodgement on a Miran ship, and crushed in a metal wall, to be stopped by a bulkhead.

The Chief engineer watched his power declining. All ten UV beams were united in one now, driving a terrible sword of energy that made the attacked ship skip for safety instantly, yet the beams were all but useless. For the Miran reserves filled the gap, and the magnetic tornado continued.

For seventeen long minutes the station resisted the attack. Then the last of the strained mercury flowed into the receivers, and the vast power of the atostors was exhausted. Slowly the magnetic fields declined. The great walls of the station felt the clutching lines of force—they began to heat and to strain. A low, harsh grinding became audible over the roar of the atomic bombs. The whole structure trembled, and jumped slightly. The roar of bombs ceased suddenly, as the station jerked again, more violently. Then it turned a bit, rolled clumsily. Abruptly it began to spin violently, more and more rapidly. It started rolling clumsily across the plateau...

A rain of atomic bombs struck the unprotected metal, and the eighth breached the walls. The twentieth was the last. There was no longer an I.P. station on Europa.

"The difference," said Buck Kendall slowly, when the reports came in from scout-ships in space that had witnessed the last struggle, "between an atomic generator and an atomic power-store, or accumulator, is clearly shown. We haven't an adequate *source* of power."

McLaurin sighed slowly, and rose to his feet. "What can we do?"

"Thank our lucky stars that Faragaut here, and I, bought up all the mercury in the system, and had it brought to Earth. We at least have a supply of materials for the atostors."

"They don't seem to do much good."

"They're the best we've got. All the photocells on Earth and Venus and Mercury are at present busy storing the sun's power in atostors. I have two thousand tons of charged mercury in our tanks here in the 'Lunar Bank.'"

"Much good that will do—they can just pull and pull and pull till it's all gone. A starfish isn't strong, but he can open the strongest oyster just because he can pull from now on. You may have a lot of power—but."

"But—we also have those new fifteen-foot UV beams. And one fifteen-foot UV beam is worth, theoretically, nine five-foot beams, and practically, a dozen. We have a dozen of them. Remember, this place was designed not only to protect itself, but Earth, too."

"They can still pull, can't they?"

"They'll stop pulling when they get their fingers burned. In the meantime, why not use some of those I.P. ships to bring in a few more cargoes of charged mercury?"

"They aren't good for much else, are they? I wonder if those fellows have anything more we don't know?"

"Oh, probably. I'm going to work on that crumbler thing. That's the first consideration now."

"Why?"

"So we can move a ship. As it is, even those two we built aren't any good."

"Would they be anyway?"

"Well—I think I might disturb those gentlemen slightly. Remember, they each have a nose-beam eighteen feet across. Exceedingly unpleasant customers."

"Score: Strangers; magnetic field, atomic bombs, atomic power, crumbler ray. Home team; UV beams."

Kendall grinned. "I'd heard you were a pessimistic cuss when battle started—"

"Pessimistic, hell, I'm merely counting things up."

"McClellan had all the odds on Lee back in the Civil War of the States—but Lee sent him home faster than he came."

"But Lee lost in the end."

"Why bring that up? I've got work to do." Still smiling, Kendall went to the laboratory he had built up in the "Lunar Bank." Devin was already there, calculating. He looked unhappy.

"We can't do anything, as far as I can see. They're using an electric field all right, and projecting it. I can't see how we can do that."

"Neither can I," agreed Kendall, "so we can't use that weapon. I really didn't want to anyway. Like the neutron gun which I told Commander McLaurin would be useless as a weapon, they'd be prepared for it, you can be sure. All I want to do is fight it, and make their projection useless."

"Well, we have to know how they project it before we can break up the projection, don't we?"

"Not at all. They're using an electric field of very high frequency, but variable frequency. As far as I can see, all we need is a similar variable electric field of a slightly different frequency to heterodyne theirs into something quite harmless."

"Oh," said Devin. "We could, couldn't we? But how are you going to do that?"

"We'll have to learn, that's all."

Buck Kendall started trying to learn. In the meantime, the Mirans were taking over Jupiter. There were three I.P. stations on the planet itself, but they were vastly hindered by the thick, almost ultra-violet-proof atmosphere of Jupiter. Their rays were weak. And the magnetic fields of the Mirans were unaffected. Only their atomic bombs were hindered by the heavier gravity that pulled the rocks back in place faster than the bombs could throw them out. Still—a few hours of work, and the I.P. stations on Jupiter had rolled wildly across the flat plains of the planet like dented cans, to end in utter destruction.

The Mirans had paid no attention to the fleeing passenger and freighter ships that left the planet, loaded to the utmost with human cargo, and absolutely no freight. The I.P. fleet had to go to their rescue with oxygen tanks to take care of the extra humans, but nearly three-quarters of the population of Jupiter, a newly established population, and hence a readily mobile one, was saved. The others, the Mirans did not bother with particularly except when they happened to be near where the Mirans wanted to work. Then they were instantly destroyed by atomic bombing, or gamma rays.

The Mirans settled almost at once, and began their work of finding on Jupiter the badly needed atomic fuels. Machines were set up, and work begun, Mirans laboring under the gravity of the heavy planet. Then, fifty ships swam up again, reloaded with fuel, and with crews consisting solely of uninjured warriors, and started for Mars.

Mars was half way between her near conjunction and her maximum elongation with respect to Jupiter at that time. The Mirans knew their business though, for they started in on the I.P. station on Phobos. They were practiced by this time, and this I.P. station had only seven five-foot beams. In half an hour that station fell, and its sister station on Deimos followed. Three wounded ships returned to Jupiter, and ten new ships came out. The attack on Mars itself was started.

Mars was a different proposition. There were thirty-two I.P. stations here, one of them nearly as powerful as the Lunar Bank station. It was equipped with four of the huge fifteen-foot beams. And it had fifteen tons of mercury, more than seven-eighths charged. The Mars Center Station was located a short ten miles from the Mars Center City, and under the immediate orders of the I.P. heads, Mars Center City had been vacated.

For two days the Mirans hung off Mars, solidifying their positions on Phobos and Deimos. Then, with sixty-two ships, they attacked. They had made some very astute observations, and they started on the smaller stations just beyond the range of the Mars Center Station. Naturally, near so powerful a center, these stations had never been strong. They fell rapidly. But they had been counted on by Mars Center as auxiliary supports. McLaurin had sent very definite orders to Mars Center forbidding any action on their part, save gathering of power-supplies.

At last the direct attack on Mars Center was launched. For the first time, the Mirans saw one of the fifteen-foot beams. Mars' atmosphere is thin, and there is little ozone. The ultra-violet beams were nearly as effective as in empty space. When the Mirans dropped their ships, a full thirty of them, into the circle formation, Mars Center answered at once. All four beams started.

Those fifteen-foot beams, connected directly to huge atostor release apparatus, delivered a maximum power of two and three-quarter billion horsepower, each. The first Miran ship struck, sparkled magnificently, and a terrific cascade of white-hot metal rolled down from its nose. The great ship nosed down and to the left abruptly, accelerated swiftly—and crashed with tremendous energy on the plain outside of Mars Center City. White, unwavering flames licked up suddenly, and made a column five hundred feet high against the dark sky. Then the wreck exploded with a violence that left a crater half a mile across.

Three other ships had been struck, and were rapidly retreating. Another try was made for the ring formation, and four more ships were wounded, and replaced. The ring did not retreat, but the great magnetic field started. Atomic and gamma ray bombs started now, flashing sometimes dangerously close to the station as its magnetic field battled the rotating field of the ships. The four greater beams, and many smaller ones were in swift and angry action. Not more than a ten-second exposure could be endured by any one ship, before it must retreat.

For five minutes the Mirans hung doggedly at their task. Then, wisely, they retreated. Of the fleet, not more than seven ships remained untouched. Mars Center Station had held—at what cost only they knew. Five hundred tons of their mercury had been exhausted in that brief five minutes. One hundred tons a minute had flowed into and out of the atostor apparatus. Mars Center radioed for help, when the fleet lifted.

There was one other station on Mars that stood a good chance of survival, Deenmor Station, with three of the big beams installed, and apparatus for their fourth was in the station, and being rapidly worked over. McLaurin did a wise and courageous thing, at which every man on Mars cursed. He ordered that all I.P. stations save these two be deserted, and all mercury fuel reserves be moved to Deenmor and Mars Center.

The Mirans could not land on the North Western section of Mars, nor in the South Central region. Therefore Mars was not exactly habitable to Miran ships, because the great beams had been so perfectly figured that they were effective at a range of nearly twelve hundred miles.

Deenmor station was attacked—but it was a half-hearted attack, for Mirans were becoming distinctly skittish about fifteen-foot UV beams. Two badly blistered ships— and the Mirans retreated to Jupiter. But Mira held Phobos and Deimos. In two weeks, they had set up cannon there, and proved themselves accurate long-range gunners. Against the feeble attraction of Deimos, and with Mars' gravity to help them, they began bombarding the two stations, and anything that attempted to approach them, with gamma and atomic explosive bombs. Meanwhile they amused themselves occasionally by planting a gamma-ray bomb in each of Mars' major cities. They made Mars uninhabitable for Solarians as well as for Mirans, at least until the deadly slow-action atomic explosives wore off, or were removed.

Then the Mirans, after a lapse of three weeks while they dug in their toes on Jupiter, prepared to leap. Earth was the next goal. Miran scout-ships had been sent out before this—and severely handled by the concentrated fleets of the I.P. that hung grimly off Earth and Luna now. But the scouts had learned one thing. Mirans could never hope to attain a firm grasp on Earth while terribly armed Luna hung like a Sword of Damocles over their heads. Further, attack on Earth directly would be next to impossible, for, thanks to Faragaut's Interplanetary Company, nearly all the mercury metal in the system was safely lodged on Earth, and saturated with power. Every major city had been equipped with great UV apparatus. And neutron guns in plenty waited on small ships just outside the atmosphere to explode harmlessly any atomic or gamma bombs Miran ships might attempt to deposit.

An attack on Luna was the first step. But that terrible, gigantic fort on Luna worried them. Yet while that fort existed, Earth ships were free to come and go, for Mirans could not afford to stand near. At a distance of twenty thousand miles, small Miran ships had felt the touch of those great UV beams.

Finally, a brief test-attack was made, with an entire fleet of one hundred ships. They drew almost into position, faster than light, faster than the signaling warnings could send their messages. In position, all those great ships strained and heaved at the mighty magnetic vortex that twisted at the field of the fort. Instantly, twelve of the fifteen-foot UV beams replied. And—two great UV beams of a size the Mirans had never seen before, beams from the two ships, "S Doradus" and "Cepheid."

The test-attack dissolved as suddenly as it had come. The Mirans returned to Jupiter, and to the outer planets where they had further established themselves. Most of the Solar system was theirs. But the Solarians still held the choicest planets—and kept the Mirans from using the mild-temperatured Mars.

CHAPTER NINE

"They can't take this, at least," sighed McLaurin as they retreated from Luna.

"I didn't think they could—right away. I'm wondering though if they haven't something we haven't seen yet. Besides which—give them time, give them time."

"Well, give us time, too," snapped McLaurin. "How are you coming?"

Buck smiled. "I'm sure I don't know. I have a machine but I haven't the slightest idea of whether or not it's any good."

"Why not?"

"I can destroy—I hope—but I can't build up their ray. I can't test the machine because I haven't their ray to test it against."

"What can we do to test it?"

"The only thing I can see is to call for volunteers—and send out a six-man cruiser. If the ship's too small, they may not destroy it with the big crumbler rays. If it's too large—and the machine didn't work—we'd lose too much."

Twelve hours later, the I.P. men at the Lunar Bank fort were lined up. McLaurin stepped up on the platform, and addressed the men briefly, told them what was needed. Six volunteers were selected by a process of elimination, those who were married, had dependents, officers, and others were refused. Finally, six men of the I.P. were chosen, neither rookies nor veterans, six average men. And one average six-man cruiser, one hundred and eleven feet long, twenty-two in diameter. It was the T-208, a sister ship of the T-247, the first ship to be destroyed.

The T-208 started out from Luna, and with full acceleration, sped out toward Phobos. Slowly she circled the satellite, while distant scouts kept her under view. Lazily, the Miran patrol on Phobos watched the T-208, indifferent to her. The T-208 dove suddenly, after five fruitless circles of the tiny world, and with her four-foot UV beam flaming, stabbed angrily at a flight of Miran scouts berthed in the very shadow of a great battle cruiser, one of the interstellar ships stationed here on Phobos.

Four of the little ships slumped in incandescence. Angrily the terrific sword of energy slashed at the frail little scouts.

Angrily the Miran interstellar ship shot herself abruptly into action against this insolent cruiser. The cruiser launched a flight of the mercury-torpedoes. Flashing, burning, ultra-violet energy flooded the great ship, harmlessly, for the men were, as usual, protected. The Miran answered with the neutron beam, atomic and gamma bombs—and the crumbler ray.

Gently, softly a halo of shimmering-violet luminescence built up about the T-208. The UV beam continued to flare, wavering slightly in its aim—then fell way off to one side. The T-208 staggered suddenly, wandered from her course—whole, but uncontrolled. For the men within the ship were dead.

Majestically the Miran swung along beside the dead ship, a great magnetic tow-cable shot out toward it, to shy off at first, then slowly to be adjusted, and take hold in the magnetic shield of the T-208. The pilots of the watching scout-ships turned away. They knew what would happen.

It did. Five—ten—twenty seconds passed. Then the "dead-man" took over the ship—and the stored power in the atostor tanks blasted in a terrible flame that shattered the metal hull to molecular fragments. The interstellar cruiser shuddered, and rolled half over at the blasting pressure. Leaking seams appeared in her plates.

The scouts raced back to Luna as the Miran settled heavily, and a trifle clumsily to Phobos. Miran radio-beams were forcing their way out toward the Miran station on Europa, to be relayed to the headquarters on Jupiter, just as Solarian radio beams were thrusting through space toward Luna. Said the Miran messages: "Their ships no longer crumble." Said the Solarian messages: "The ships no longer crumble—but the men die."

His deep eyes burning tensely, Buck Kendall heard the messages coming in, and rose slowly from his seat to pace the floor. "I think I know why," he said at last. "I should have thought. For that too can be prevented."

"Why—what in the name of the Planets?" asked McLaurin. "It didn't kill the men in the forts—why does it kill the men in the ships, when the ships are protected?"

"The protection kills them."

"But—but they had the protective oscillations on all the way out!" protested the Commander.

"Think how it works though. Think, man. The enemy's field is an electric-field oscillation. We combat it by setting up a similar oscillating field in the metal of the hull ourselves. Because the metal conducts the strains, they meet, and oppose. It is not a shield—a shield is impossible, as I have said, because of energy concentration factors. If their beam carried a hundred thousand horsepower in a ten-foot square beam, in every ten square feet of our shield, we'd have to have one hundred thousand horsepower. In other words, hundreds of times as much energy would be needed in the shield, as they used in their beam. We can't afford that. We had to let the beams oppose our oscillations in the metal, where, because the metal conducts, they meet on an equal basis. But—when two oscillations of slightly different frequency meet, what is the result?"

"In this case, a heterodyne frequency of a lower, and harmless frequency."

"So I thought. I was partly right. It does *not* harm the metal. But it kills the men. It is super-sonic. The terrible, shrill sounds destroy the cells of the men's bodies. Then, when their dead hands release the controls, the automatic switches blow up the ship."

"God! We stop one menace—and it is like the Hydra. For every head we lop off, two spring up."

"Ah—but they are lesser heads. Look, what is the fundamental difference between sound and light?"

"One is a vibration of matter and the—ah—eliminate the material contact!"

"Exactly! All we need to do is to let the ships operate airless, the men in space suits. Then the air cannot carry the sounds to them. And by putting special damping materials in their suits, we can stop the vibrations that would reach them through their feet and hands. Another six-man ship must go out—but this ship will come back!"

And with the order for another experimental ship, went the orders for commercial supplies of this new apparatus. Every I.P. ship must be equipped to resist it.

Buck Kendall sailed on the six-man scout that went out this time. Again they swooped once at Phobos, again Miran scout-ships crumbled under the attack of the vicious UV beams. The Mirans were not waiting contemptuously this time. In an instant the great interstellar ship rose from its berth, its weapons working angrily. The crumbler ray snapped out at the T-253.

Kendall stared into the periscope visor intently. Clumsily his padded hands worked at the specially adapted controls. The soft hiss of the oxygen release into his suit disturbed him slightly. The radio-phones in his helmet carried all the conversations in the ship to him with equal clarity. He watched as the great ship angled angrily up...

His vision was momentarily obscured by a violet glow that built up and reached out gently from every point of metal in the ship. The instant Kendall saw that, the T-253 was fleeing under his hands. The test had been made. Now all he desired was safety again. The ion-rockets flared recklessly as, crushed under an acceleration of four Earth-gravities, he sank heavily into his seat. Grimly the Miran ship was pursuing them, easily keeping up with the fleeing midget. The crumbler became more intense, the violet glow more vivid.

The UV beam was reaching out directly behind now. The...

With a cry of agony, Kendall ripped the radio-phone connection out of his suit. A soft hiss of leaking air warned him of too great violence only minutes later. For his ears had been deafened by the sudden shriek of a tremendous signal from outside!

Instantly Kendall knew what that meant. And he could not communicate with his men! There was no metal in these special suits, even the oxygen tanks were made of synthetic plastics of tremendous strength. No scrap of vibrating metal was permissible. The padded gloves and boots protected him—but there was a new and different type of crackle and haze from the metal points now. It was almost invisible in the practically airless ship, but Kendall saw it.

Presently he felt it, as he desperately increased his acceleration. Slow creeping heat was attacking him. The heat was increasing rapidly now. Desperately he was working at the crumbler-protection controls—but immediately set them back as they were. He had to have the crumbler protection as well!

Grimly the great Miran ship hung right beside them. Angrily the two four-foot UV beams flashed back— seeking some weak spot. There were none. At her absolute maximum of acceleration the little ship plunged on. Gamma and atomic bombs were washing her in flame. The heavy blocks of paraffin between her walls were long since melted, retained only by the presence of the metal walls. Smoke was beginning to filter out now, and Kendall recognized a new, and deadlier menace! Heat—quantities of heat were being poured into the little ship, and the neutron guns were doing their best to add to it. The paraffin was confined in there—and like any substance, it could be volatilized, and as a vapor, develop pressure— explosive pressure!

The Miran seemed satisfied in his tactics so far—and changed them. Forty-seven million miles from Earth, the Miran simply accelerated a bit more, and crowded the Solarian ship a bit. White-faced, Buck Kendall was forced to turn a bit aside. The Miran turned also. Kendall turned a bit more...

Flashing across his range of vision at an incredible speed, a tiny thing, no more than twenty feet long and five in diameter, a scout-ship appeared. Its tiny nose ultra-violet beam was blasting a solid cylinder of violet incandescence a foot across in the hull of the Miran—and, to the Miran, angling swiftly across his range of vision. Its magnetic field clashed for a thousandth of a second with the T-253, instantly meeting, and absorbing the fringing edges. Then—it swept through the Miran's magnetic shield as easily. The delicate instruments of the scout instantaneously adjusted its own magnetic field as much as possible. There was resistance, enormous resistance—the ship crumpled in on itself, the tail vanished in dust as a sweeping crumbler beam caught it at last—and the remaining portion of the ship plowed into the nose of the Miran.

The Miran's force-control-room was wrecked. For perhaps a minute and a half, the ship was without control, then the control was re-established—and in vain the telescopes and instruments searched for the T-253. Lightless, her rockets out now, her fields damped down to extinction, the T-253 was lost in the pulsing, gyrating fields of half a dozen scout-ships.

Kendall looked grimly at the crushed spot on the nose of the Miran. His ship was drifting slowly away from the greater ship. Presently, however, the Miran put on speed in the direction of Earth, and the T-253 fell far behind. The Miran was not seriously injured. But that scout pilot, in sacrificing life, had thrown dust in their eyes for just those few moments Kendall had needed to lose a lightless ship in lightless space—lightless—for the Mirans at any rate. The I.P. ships had been covered with a black paint, and in no time at all, Kendall had gotten his ship into a position where the energy radiations of the sun made him undetectable from the Miran's position, since the radiation of his own ship, even in the heat range, was mingled with the direct radiation of the sun. The sun was in the Miran's "eyes," both actual and instrumental.

An hour later the Miran returned, passed the still-lightless ship at a distance of five million miles, and settled to Phobos for the slight repairs needed.

Twelve hours later, the T-253 settled to Luna, for the many rearrangements she would need.

"I rather knew it was coming," Kendall admitted sadly, "but danged if I didn't forget all about it. And—cost the life of one of the finest men in the system. Jehnson's family get a permanent pension just twice his salary, McLaurin. In the meantime—"

"What was it? Pure heat, but how?"

"Pure radio. Nothing but short-wave radio directed at us. They probably had the apparatus, knew how to make it, but that's not a good type of heat ray, because a radio tube is generally less than eighty percent efficient, which is a whale of a loss when you're working in a battle, and a whale of an inconvenience. We were heated only four times as much as the Miran. He had to pump that heat into a heat-reservoir—a water tank probably—to protect himself. Highly inefficient and ineffective against a large ship. Also, he had to hold his beam on us nearly ten minutes before it would have become unbearable. He was again, trying to kill the men, and not the ship. The men are the weakest point, obviously."

"Can you overcome that?"

"Obviously, no. The thing works on pure energy. I'd have to match his energy to neutralize it. You knew it's an old proposition, that if you could take a beam of pure, monochromatic light and divide it exactly in half, and then recombine it in perfect interference, you'd have annihilation of energy. Cancellation to extinction. The trouble is, you never do get that. You can't get monochromatic light, because light can't be monochromatic. That's due to the Heisenberg Uncertainty—my pet bug-bear. The atom that radiates the light, must be moving. If it isn't, the emission of the light itself gives it a kick that moves it. Now, no matter what the quantum *might* have been, it loses energy in kicking the atom. That changes the situation instantly, and incidentally the 'color' of the light. Then, since all the radiating atoms won't be moving alike, etc., the mass of light can't be monochromatic. Therefore perfect interference is impossible.

"The way that relates to the problem in hand, is that we can't possibly destroy his energy. We can, as we do in the crumbler stunt, change it. He can't, I suspect, put too much power behind his crumbler, or he'd have crumbling going on at home. We get a slight heating from it, anyway. Into the bargain, his radio was after us, and his neutrons naturally carried energy. Now, no matter what we do, we've got that to handle. When we fight his crumbler, we actually add heat-energy to it, ourselves, and make the heating effect just twice as bad. If we try to heterodyne his radio—presto—it has twice the heat energy anyway, though we might reduce it to a frequency that penetrated the ship instead of all staying in it. But by the proposition, we have to use as much energy, and in fact, remember the 80% rule. We've got to take it and like it."

"But," objected McLaurin, "we *don't* like it."

"Then build ships as big as his, and he'll quit trying to roast you. Particularly if the inner walls are synthetic plastics. Did you know I used them in the 'S Doradus' and 'Cepheid'?"

"Yes. Were you thinking of that?"

"No—just luck—and the fact that they're light, strong as steel almost, and can be manufactured in forms much more quickly. Only the outer hull is tungsten-beryllium. The advantage in this will be that nearly all the energy will be absorbed outside, and we'll radiate pretty fast, particularly as that tungsten-beryllium has a high radiation-factor in the long heat range."

"What does that mean?"

"Well, ordinary polished silver is a mighty poor radiator. Homely example: Try waiting for your coffee to cool if it's in a polished silver pot. Then try it in a tungsten-beryllium pot. No matter how you polish that tungsten-beryllium, the stuff WILL radiate heat. That's why an I.P. ship is always so blamed cold. You know the passenger ships use polished aluminum outer walls. The big help is, that the tungsten-beryllium will throw off the energy pretty fast, and in a big ship, with a whale of a lot of matter to heat, the Strangers will simply give up the idea."

"Yes, but only two ships in the system compare with them in size."

"Sorry—but I didn't build the I.P. fleet, and there are lots of tungsten and beryllium on Earth. Enough anyway."

"Will they use that beam on the fort? And can't we use the thing on them?"

"They won't and we won't—though we could. A bank of those new million watt tubes—perhaps a hundred of them—and we'd have a pretty effective heater—but an awful waste of power. I've got something better."

"New?"

"Somewhat. I've found out how to make the mirror field in a plate of metal, instead of a block. Come on to the lab, and I'll show you."

"What's the advantage? Oh—weight saved, and silver metal saved."

"A lot more than that, Mac. Watch."

At the laboratory, the new apparatus looked immensely lighter and simpler than the old. The atostor, the ionizer, and the twin ion-projectors were as before, great, rigid, metal structures that would maintain the meeting point of the ions with inflexible exactitude under any acceleration strains. But now, instead of the heavy silver block in which a mirror was figured, the mirror consisted of a polished silver plate, parabolic to be sure, but little more than a half-inch in thickness. It was mounted in a framework of complex, stout metal braces.

Kendall started the ion-flame at low intensity, so the UV beam was little more than a spotlight.

"You missed the point, Mac. Now—watch that tungsten-beryllium plate. I'll hold the power steady. It's an eighteen-inch beam—and now the energy is just sufficient to heat that tungsten plate to bright red. But—"

Kendall turned over a small rheostat control—and abruptly the eighteen-inch diameter spot on the tungsten-beryllium plate began contracting; it contracted till it was a blazing, sparkling spot of molten incandescence less than an inch across!

"That's the advantage of focus. At this distance of a few hundred feet with a small beam I can do that. With a twenty-foot beam, I can get a two-foot spot at a distance of nearly ten miles! That means that the receiving end will have the pleasure of handling *one hundred times the energy concentration*. That would punch a hole through most anything. All you have to do is focus it. The trouble being, if it's out of focus the advantage is more than lost. So if there's any question about getting the focus, we'll get along without it."

"A real help, if you do. That would punch a hole before the Stranger ship could turn away as they do now."

Kendall nodded. "That's what I was after. It is mainly for the forts, though. We'll have to signal the dope to the Mars Center and Deenmor stations. They can fix it up, themselves. In the meantime—all we can do is hold on and hunt, and let's hope better than the Strangers do."

CHAPTER TEN

Sadly the convalescent Gresth Gkae listened to the reports of his lieutenants. More and more disgraced he felt as he realized how badly he had blundered in reporting the people of this system unable to cope with the attackers' weapons. Gresth Gkae looked up at his old friend and physician, Merth Skahl. He shook his head slowly. "I'm afraid, Merth Skahl. I am afraid. We have, perhaps, made a mistake. The better and the stronger alone should rule. Aye, but is the *stronger* always the *better*? I am afraid we have mistaken the Truth in assuming this. If we have— then may Jarth, Lord of Truth and Wisdom punish us. Mighty Jarth, if I have mistaken in following my judgments, it is not from disobedience, it is lack of Thy knowledge. The strongest—they are not always the better, are they?"

Merth Skahl bent sharply over his friend. "Quiet thyself, Gresth Gkae. You know, and I know, you have done only your best, and surely Jarth himself can ask no better of any one. You must rest, for only by rest can those terrible burns be healed. All your *stheen* over half the body-area was burned off. You have been delirious for many days."

"But Merth Skahl, think—have we disobeyed Jarth's will? It is, we know, his will that only the best and the strongest shall rule—but are the best always the strongest? An imbecile adult could destroy the life of a genius-grade child. The strongest wins, but not the best. Such would not be the will of Jarth. If we be the stronger, *and* the best, then it is right and just that these strange creatures should be destroyed that we may have a stable world of stable light and heat. But look and see, with what terrible swiftness these strange creatures have learned! May it not be they are the better race—that it is *we* who are the weaker and the poorer? Can it be that Jarth has brought us together that these people might learn—and destroy us? If they be the stronger, and the better—then may Jarth's will be done. But we must test our strength to the utmost. I must rise, and go to my laboratory soon. They have set it up?"

"Aye, they have, Gresth Gkae. But remember, the weak and the sick make faults the strong and the well do not. Better that you rest yourself. There is little you can do while your body seeks to recover from these terrible burns."

"You are wrong, my friend, wrong. Don't you see that my mind is clear—that it is the mind which must fight in these battles, for surely the man is weak against such things as this infra-X-radiation? Why, I am better able to fight now than are you, for I am a trained fighter of the mind, while you are a trained healer of the body. These strange beings with their stiff arms and legs, their tender skins, and—and their swift minds have fought us all too well. If we must test, let it be a test. I have heard how they so quickly solved the riddle of the crumbling field. That took us longer, and we designed it. The Counsel of Worlds put me in command, let me up, Skahl, I must work."

Concerned, the physician looked down at him. Finally he spoke again. "No, I will not permit you to leave the hospital-ship. You must stay here, but if, as you have said, the mind is what must fight, then surely you can fight well from here, for your mind is here."

"No, I cannot, and you well know it. I may shorten my life, but what matter. 'Death is the end toward which the chemical reaction, Life, tends,'" quoted the scientist. "You know I have left my children—my immortality is assured through them. I can afford to die in peace, if it assures their welfare. Time is precious, and while my mind might work from here, it must have data on which to work. For that, I must go to the laboratories. Help me, Merth Skahl."

Reluctantly the physician granted the request, but begged of Gresth Gkae a promise of at least six hours rest in every fifteen, and a good sleep of at least twenty-seven hours every "night." Gresth Gkae agreed, and from a wheelchair, conducted his work, began a new line of experimentation he hoped would yield them the weapon they needed. Under him, the staff of scientists worked, aiding and advising and suggesting. The apparatus was built, tested, and found wanting. Time and again as the days passed, they watched Gresth Gkae, gaining strength very, very slowly, taken away despondent at the end of his forty hours of work.

A dozen expeditions were sent to Jupiter's poles to watch and measure and study the tremendous auroral displays there, where Jupiter's vast magnetic field sucked in countless quintillions of the flying electrons from the sun, and brought them circling in, in a vast, magnificent display of auroral ionization.

Expeditions went to the great Southern Plateau, the Plateau of Storms, where the titanic air currents resulted in an everlasting display of terrific lightnings, great burning balls of electric force floating dangerous and deadly across the frozen, ultra-cold plain.

And the expeditions brought back data. Yet still Gresth Gkae could not sleep, his thoughts intruding constantly. Hours Merth Skahl spent with him, calming him to sleep.

"But what is this constant search? It is little enough I know of science, but why do you send our men to these spots of wonderfully beautiful, but useless natural forces. Can we somehow, do you think, turn them against the people of these worlds?"

Softly the old Miran smiled. "Yes, you might say so. For look, it is the strange balls of electric force I want to know about. Sthor had few, but occasionally we saw them. Never were they properly investigated. I want to know their secret, for I am sure they are balls of electric forces not vastly dissimilar from the nucleus of the atom. Always we have known that no system of purely electrical forces could remain stable. Yet these strange balls of energy do. How is it? I am sure it will be of vast importance. But the direct secret I hope to learn is in this: What can be done with electric fields can nearly always be duplicated, or paralleled in magnetic fields. If I can learn how to make these electric balls of energy, can I not hope to make similar magnetic balls of energy?"

"Yes, I see—that would seem true. But what benefit would you derive from that? You have magnetic beams now, and yet they are useless because you can get nowhere near the forts. How then would these benefit you?"

"We can do nothing to those forts, because of that magnetic shield. Could we once break it down, then the fort is helpless, and one or two small atomic bombs destroy it. But—we cannot stay near, for the terrible infra-X-rays of theirs burn holes in our ships, and—in our men.

"But look you, I can drop many atomic bombs from a distance where their beams are ineffective. Suppose I *do* make a magnetic ball of energy, a magnetic bomb. Then— I can drop it from a distance! We have learned that the power supply of these forts is very great—but not endless, as is ours now, thanks to the vast supplies of power metal on this heavy planet. Then all we need do is stay at a distance where they cannot reach us—and drop magnetic bombs. Ah, they will be stopped, and their energy absorbed. But we can keep it up, day after day, and slowly drain out their power. Then—then our atomic bombs can destroy those forts, and we can move on!" But suddenly the animation and strength left his voice. He turned a sad, downcast face to his friend. "But Merth Skahl, we can't do it," he complained.

"Ah—now I can see why you so want to continue this wearing and worrying work. You need time, Gresth Gkae, only time for success. Tomorrow it may be that you will see the first hint that will lead you to success."

"Ah—I only hope it, Merth Skahl, I only hope it."

But it was the next day that they saw the first glimpse of the secret, and saw the path that might lead to hope and success. In a week they were sending electric bombs across the laboratory. And in three days more, a magnetic bomb streaked dully across the laboratory to a magnetic shield they had set up, and buried itself in it, to explode in brilliant light and heat.

From that day Gresth Gkae began to mend. In the three weeks that were needed to build the apparatus into ships, he regained strength so that when the first flight of five interstellar ships rose from Jupiter, he was on the flagship.

To Phobos they went first, to the little inner satellite of Mars, scarcely eight miles in diameter, a tiny bit of broken metal and rock, utterly airless, but scarcely more than 3700 miles from the surface of Mars below. The Mars Center and Deenmor forts were wasting no power raying a ship at that distance. They could, of course, have damaged it, but not severely enough to make up for the loss of their strictly limited power. The photocells had been working overtime, every minute of available light had been used, and still scarcely 2100 tons of charged mercury remained in the tanks of Mars Center and 1950 in the tanks at Deenmor.

The flight of five ships settled comfortably upon Phobos, while the three relieved of duty started back to Jupiter. Immediately work was begun on the attack. The ships were first landed on the near side, while the apparatus of the projectors was unloaded, then the great ships moved around to the far side. Phobos of course rotated with one face fixed irrevocably toward Mars itself, the other always to the cold of space. Great power leads trailed beneath the ships, and to the dark side. Then there were huge water lines for cooling. On this almost weightless world, where the great ships weighing hundreds of thousands of tons on a planet, weighed so little they were frequently moved about by a single man, the laying of five miles of water conduit was no impossibility.

Then they were ready. Mars Center came first. Automatic devices kept the aim exact, as the first of the magnetic bombs started down. At five-second intervals they were projected outward, invisible globes of concentrated magnetic energy, undetectable in space. Seven seconds passed before the first became dimly visible in the thin air of Mars. It floated down, it would miss the fort it seemed…so far to one side… Abruptly it turned, and darted with tremendously accelerating speed for the great magnetic field of the fort. With a vast blast of light, it exploded. Five seconds later a second exploded. And a third.

Mars Center signaled scoffingly that the bombs were all being stopped dead in the magnetic atmosphere, after the bombardment had been witnessed from Earth and Luna. An hour later they gave a report that they were concentrated magnetic fields of energy that would be rather dangerous—if it weren't that they couldn't even stand into the magnetic atmosphere. Three hours later Mars Center reported that they contained considerably more energy than had at first been thought. Further, which they had not carefully considered at first, they were taking energy with them! They were taking away about an equal amount of energy as each blew up.

It was only a half-hour after that that the men at Mars Center realized perfectly what it meant. Their power was being drained just a little bit better than twice as fast as they generated during the day—and since Phobos spun so swiftly across the sky.

Deenmor got the attack just about the time Mars Center was released. Deenmor immediately began seeking for the source of it. Somewhere on Phobos—but where?

The Mirans were experts at camouflage. Deenmor Station, realizing the menace, immediately rayed the "projector." They tore up a great deal of harmless rock with their huge UV rays. But the bomb device continued to throw one bomb each five seconds.

When Deenmor operated from Phobos' position, Mars Center was exposed to the deadly, constant drain. A day or two later, the bombs were coming one each second and a half, for more ships had joined in the work on Phobos.

Gresth Gkae saw the work was going nicely. He knew that now it was only a question of time before those magnetic shields would fail—and then the whole fort would be powerless. Maybe—it might be a good idea, when the forts were powerless to investigate instead of blowing them up. There might be many interesting and worthwhile pieces of apparatus—particularly the UV beam's apparatus.

CHAPTER ELEVEN

Buck Kendall entered the Communications room rather furtively. He hated the place. Cole was there, and McLaurin. Mac was looking tired and drawn, Cole not so tired, but equally drawn. The signals were coming through fairly well, because most of the disturbance was rising where the signals rose, and all the disturbance, practically, was magnetic rather than electric.

"Deenmor is sending, Buck," McLaurin said as he entered. "They're down to the last fifty-five tons. They'll have more time now—a rest while Phobos sinks. Mars Center has another 250 tons, but—it's just a question of time. Have you any hope to offer?"

"No," said Kendall in a strained voice. "But, Mac, I don't think men like those are afraid to die. It's dying uselessly they fear. Tell 'em—tell 'em they've defended not alone Mars, but all the system, in holding up the Strangers on Mars. We here on Luna have been safer because of them. And tell—Mac, tell them that in the meantime, while they defended us, and gave us time to work, we have begun to see the trail that will lead to victory."

"*You have!*" gasped McLaurin.

"No—but they will never know!" Kendall left hastily. He went and stood moodily looking at the calculator machines—the calculator machines that refused to give the answers he sought. No matter how he might modify that original idea of his, no matter what different line of attack he might try in solving the problems of Space and Matter, while he used the system he *knew* was right—the answer came down to that deadly, hope-blasting expression that meant only "uncertain."

Even Buck was beginning to feel uncertain under that constant crushing of hope. Uncertainty—uncertainty was eating into him, and destroying…

From the Communications room came the hum and drive of the great sender flashing its message across seventy-two millions of miles of nothing. *"B-u-c-k K-e-n-d-a-l-l s-a-y-s h-e h-a-s l-e-a-r-n-e-d s-o-m-e-t-h-i-n-g t-h-a-t w-i-l-l l-e-a-d t-o v-i-c-t-o-r-y w-h-i-l-e y-o-u h-e-l-d b-a-c-k t-h-e—"*

Kendall switched on a noisy, humming fan viciously. The too-intelligible signals were drowned in its sound.

"And—tell them to—destroy the apparatus before the last of the power is gone," McLaurin ordered softly.

The men in Deenmor station did slightly better than that. Gradually they cut down their magnetic shield, and some of the magnetic bombs tore and twisted viciously at the heavy metal walls. The thin atmosphere of Mars leaked in. Grimly the men waited. Atomic bombs—or ships to investigate? It did not matter much to them personally…

Gresth Gkae smiled with his old vigor as he ordered one of the great interstellar ships to land beside the powerless station, approaching from such an angle that the still-active Mars Center station could not attack. One of the fleet of Phobos rose, and circled about the planet, and settled gracefully beside the station. For half an hour it lay there quietly, waiting and watching. Then a crew of two dozen Mirans started across the dry, crumbly powder of Mars' sands, toward the fort. Simultaneously almost, three things happened. A three-foot UV beam wiped out the advancing party. A pair of fifteen-foot beams cut a great gaping hole in the wall of the interstellar ship, as it darted up, like a startled quail, its weapons roaring defiance, only to fall back, severely wounded.

And the radio messages pounded out to Earth the first description of the Miran people. Methodically the men in Deenmor station used all but one ton of their power to completely and forever wreck and destroy the interstellar cripple that floundered for a few moments on the sands a bare mile away. Presently, before Deenmor was through with it, the atomic bombs stopped coming, and the atomic shells. The magnetic shield that had been re-established for the few minutes of this last, dying sting, fell.

Deenmor station vanished in a sudden, colossal tongue of blue-green light as the ton of atomically distorted mercury was exploded by a projector beam turned on the tank.

It was long gone, when the first atomic bombs and magnetic bombs dropped from Phobos reached the spot, and only hot rock and broken metal remained.

Mars Center failed in fact the next time Phobos rode high over it. The apparatus here had been carefully destroyed by technicians with a view of making it indecipherable, but the Mirans made it even more certain, for no ship settled here to investigate, but a stream of atomic bombs that lasted for over an hour, and churned the rock to dust, and the dust to molten lava, in which pools of fused tungsten-beryllium alloy bubbled slowly and sank.

"Ah, Jarth—they are a brave race, whatever we may say of their queer shape," sighed Gresth Gkae as the last of Mars Center sank in bubbling lava. "They stung as they died." For some minutes he was silent.

"We must move on," he said at length. "I have been thinking, and it seems best that a few ships land here, and establish a fort, while some twenty move on to the satellite of the third planet and destroy the fort there. We cannot operate against the planet while that hangs above us."

Seven ships settled to Mars, while the fleet came up from Jupiter to join with Gresth Gkae's flight of ships on its way to Luna.

An automatically controlled ship was sent ahead, and began the bombardment. It approached slowly, and was not destroyed by the UV beams till it had come to within 40,000 miles of the fort. At 60,000 Gresth Gkae stationed his fleet—and returned to 150,000 immediately as the titanic UV beams of the Lunar Fort stretched out to their maximum range. The focus made a difference. One ship started limping back to Jupiter, in tow of a second, while the rest began the slow, methodical work of wearing down the defenses of the Lunar Fort.

Kendall looked out at the magnificent display of clashing, warring energies, the great, whirling spheres and discs of opalescent flame, and turned away sadly. "The men at Deenmor must have watched that for days. And at Mars Center."

"How long can we hold out?" asked McLaurin.

"Three weeks or so, at the present rate. That's a long time, really. And we can escape if we want to. The UV beams here have a greater range than any weapon the Strangers have, and with Earth so near—oh, we could escape. Little good."

"What are you going to do?"

"I," said Buck Kendall, suddenly savage, "am going to consign all the math machines in the universe to eternal damnation—and go ahead and build a machine anyway. I *know* that thing ought to be right. The math's wrong."

"There is no other thing to try?"

"A billion others. I don't know how many others. We ought to get atomic energy somehow. But that thing infuriates me. A hundred things that math has predicted, that I have checked by experiment, simple little things. But—when I carry it through to the point where I can get something useful—it wriggles off into—uncertainty."

Kendall stalked off to the laboratory. Devin was there working over the calculus machines, and Kendall called him angrily. Then more apologetic, he explained it was anger at himself. "Devin, I'm going to make that thing, if it blows up and kills me. I'm going to make that thing if this whole fort blows up and kills me. That math has blown up in my face for four solid months, and half killed me, so I'm going to kill it. Come on, we'll make that damned junk."

Angrily, furiously, Kendall drove his helpers to the task. He had worked out the apparatus in plan a dozen times, and now he had the plans turned into patterns, the patterns into metal.

Saucily, the "S Doradus" made the trip to and from Earth with patterns, and with metal, with supplies and with apparatus. But she had to dodge and fight every inch of the way as the Miran ships swooped down angrily at her. A fighting craft could get through when the Miran fleet was withdrawn to some distance, but the Mirans were careful that no heavy-loaded freighter bearing power supply should get through.

And Gresth Gkae waited off Luna in his great ship, and watched the steady streams of magnetic bombs exploding on the magnetic shield of the Lunar Fort. Presently more ships came up, and added their power to the attack, for here, the photo-cell banks could gather tremendous energy, and Gresth Gkae knew he would need to overcome this, and drain the accumulated power.

Gresth Gkae felt certain if he could once crack this nut, break down Earth, he would have the system. This was the home planet. If this fell, then the two others would follow easily, despite the fact that the few forts on the innermost planet, Mercury, could gather energy from the sun at a rate greater than their ships could generate.

It took Kendall two weeks and three days to set up his preliminary apparatus. They had power for perhaps four days more, thanks to the fact that the long Lunar day had begun shortly after Gresth Gkae's impatient attack had started. Also, the "S Doradus" had brought in several hundred tons of charged mercury on each trip, though this was no great quantity individually, it had mounted up in the ten trips she had made. The "Cepheid," her sister ship, had gone along on seven of the trips, and added to the total.

But at length the apparatus was set up. It was peculiar looking, and it employed a great deal of power, nearly as much as a UV beam in fact. McLaurin looked at it sceptically toward the last, and asked Buck: "What do you expect it to do?"

"I am," said Kendall sourly, "uncertain. The result will be uncertainty itself."

Which, considering things, was a surprisingly accurate statement. Kendall gave the exact answer. He meant to give an ironic comment. For the mathematics had been perfectly correct, only Buck Kendall misinterpreted the answer.

"I've followed the math with mechanism all the way through," he explained, "and I'm putting power into it. That's all I know. Somewhere, by the laws of cause and effect, this power *must* show itself again—despite what the damn math says."

And in that, of course, Kendall was wrong. Because the laws of cause and effect didn't hold in what he was doing now.

"Do you want to watch?" he asked at length. "I'm all set to try it."

"I suppose I may as well." McLaurin smiled. "In our close-knit little community the fate of one is of interest to all. If it's going to blow up, I might as well be here, and if it isn't, I want to be."

Kendall smiled appreciatively and replied: "Let it be on thy own head. Here she goes."

He walked over to the power board, and took command. Devin, and a squad of other scientists were seated about the room with every conceivable type and combination of apparatus. Kendall wanted to see what this was doing. "Tubes," he called. "Circuits A and D. Tie-ins." He stopped, the preliminary switches in. "Main circuit coming." With a jerk he threw over the last contact.

A heavy relay thudded solidly. The hum of a straining atostor. Then...

An electric motor, humming smoothly stopped with a jerk. "This," it remarked in a deep throaty voice, "is probably the last stand of humanity."

The galvanometer before which Devin was seated apparently agreed. In a rather high pitched voice it pointed out that: "If the Lunar Fort falls, the Earth—" It stopped abruptly, and an electroscope beside Douglass took up the thread in a high, shrill voice, rather slurred, "—will be directly attacked."

"This," resumed the motor in a hoarse voice, "will certainly mean the end of humanity." The motor gave up the discourse and hummed violently into action—in reverse!

"My God!" Kendall pulled the switch open with a sagging jaw and staring eyes.

The men in the room burst into sudden startled exclamations.

Kendall didn't give them time. His jaw snapped shut, and a blazing light of wondrous joy shone in his eyes. He instantly threw the switch in again. Again the humming atostor, the strain...

Slowly Devin lifted from his seat. With thrashing arms and startled, staring eyes, he drifted gently across the room. Abruptly he fell to the floor, unhurt by the light Lunar gravity.

"I advise," said the motor in its grumbling voice, "an immediate exodus." It stopped speaking, and practiced what it preached. It was a fifty-horse motor-generator, on a five-ton tungsten-beryllium base, but it rose abruptly, spun rapidly about an axis at right angles to the axis of its armature, and stopped as suddenly. In mid air it continued its interrupted lecture. "Mercury therefore is the destination I would advise. There power is sufficient for—all machines." Gently it inverted itself and settled to the middle of the floor. Kendall instantly cut the switch. The relay did not chunk open. It refused to obey. Settled in the middle of the floor now, torn loose from its power leads, the motor-generator began turning. It turned faster and faster. It was shrilling in a thin scream of terrific speed, a speed that should have torn its windings to fragments under the lash of centrifugal force. Contentedly it said throatily. "Settled."

The galvanometer spoke again in its peculiar harsh voice. "Therefore, move." Abruptly, without apparent reason, the stubborn relay clicked open. The shrilly screaming motor stopped dead instantly, as though it had had no real momentum, or had been inertialess.

Startled, white-faced men looked at Kendall. Buck's eyes were shining with an unholy glee.

"*Uncertainty!*" he shouted. "Uncertainty—uncertainty—uncertainty, you fools! Don't you see it? All the math—it said uncertainty—man, man—*we've got just that—uncertainty!*"

"You're crazy," gasped McLaurin. "I'm crazy, everything's gone crazy."

Kendall roared with sudden, joyous laughter. "Absolutely. Everything goes crazy—*the laws of nature break down!* Heisenberg's principle showed that the law of cause and effect weren't absolute. We've made them absolutely uncertain!"

"But—but motors *talking*, instruments giving lectures—"

"Certainly—or rather uncertainly—anything, absolutely anything. The destruction of the laws of gravity, freedom from inertia—why, merely picking up a radio lecture is nothing!"

Suddenly, abruptly, a thousand questions poured in on him. Jubilantly he answered what he could, told what he thought—and then brought order. "The battle's still on, men—we've still got to find out how to use this, now we've got it. I have an idea—that there's a lot more. I know what I'll get this time. Now help me remake this apparatus so we don't broadcast the thing."

At once, ten times the former pace, work was done. On the radio, news was sent out that Kendall was on the right track after all. In two hours the apparatus had been vastly altered, it was in the final stage, and an entirely different sort of field set up. Again they watched as Buck applied the power.

The atostor hummed—but no strange tricks of matter happened this time. The more concentrated, altered field was, as Buck was to find out later, "Uncertainty of the Second Degree." It was molecular uncertainty. In a field a foot and a half in diameter, Buck saw the thing created— and suddenly a brilliant green-blue flame shot up, and a great dark cloud of terrible, red-brown deadly vapor. Then an instant later, Kendall had opened the relay. Gasping, the men ran from the laboratory, shutting the deadly fumes in. "N_2O_4" gasped Morton, the chemist, as they reached safety. "It's exothermic—but it formed there!"

In that instant, Kendall grasped the meaning the choking fumes carried. "Molecular uncertainty!" he decided. "We're going back—we're getting there—"

He altered the apparatus again, added another atostor in series, reduced the size of his sphere of forces—of strange chaos of uncertainty. Within—little was certain. Without—the laws of nature applied as ever.

Again the apparatus was started, cautiously this time. Only a strange jumbled ionization appeared this time, then a slow, rising blue flame began to creep up, and burn hot and blue. Buck looked at it for a moment, then his face grew tense and thoughtful. "Devin—give me a half-dollar." Blankly, Devin reached in his pocket, and handed over the metal disc. Cautiously Buck Kendall tossed it toward the sphere of force. Instantly there was a flash of flame, soundless and soft-colored. Then the silver disc was outlined in light, and swiftly, inevitably crumbling into dust so fine only a blue haze appeared. In less than two seconds, the metal was gone. Only the dense blue fog remained. Then this began to go, and the leaping blue flame grew taller, and stronger.

"We're on the track—I'm going to stop here, and calculate. Bring the data—"

Kendall shut off the machine, and went to the calculation room. Swiftly he selected already prepared graphs, graphs of the math he had worked on. Devin came soon, and others. They assembled the data and with tables and arithmetical machines turned it into graphs.

Then all these graphs were fed into the machine. There were curves, and sine-curves, abrupt breaking lines—but the answer that came when all were compounded was a perfect diagram of a flight of four steps, descending in unequal treads to zero.

Kendall looked at it for long minutes. "That," he said at length, "is what I expected. There are four degrees of uncertainty, we generated 'Uncertainty of the First Degree,' 'Mass Uncertainty,' when we started. That, as here shown, takes little energy concentration. Then we increased the energy concentration and got 'Uncertainty of the Second Degree,' 'Molecular Uncertainty.' Then I added more power, and reduced the field, and got 'Uncertainty of the Third Degree'—'Atomic Uncertainty.' There is 'Uncertainty of the Fourth Degree.' It is barely attainable with our atostors. It is—utter uncertainty.

"In the First Degree, the laws of mass action fail, the great broad-reaching laws. In the Second Degree, the laws of the molecules, a finer organization, break down, and anything can happen in chemistry. In the Third Degree, the laws of atomic physics break down slowly. The atom is tough. It is very compact, and we just barely attained the concentration needed with that apparatus. But—in the Third Degree, when the Atomic Laws break down into utter uncertainty, the atoms break, and only hydrogen can exist. That was the blue flame.

"But the Fourth Degree—*there is no law whatsoever*, nothing in all the Universe can exist. It means—*the utter destruction and release of the energy of matter!*" Kendall paused for a moment. "We have won, with this. We need only make up this apparatus—and maybe make it into a weapon. You know, in the Fourth Degree, nothing in all the Universe could resist, deflect, or control it, if launched freely, and self-maintaining. I think that might be done. You see, no law affects it, for it breaks down the law. Magnetism cannot attract or repel it because magnetic fields cannot exist; there is no law of magnetic force, where this field is.

"And you know, Devin, how I have analyzed and duplicated their magnetic ball-fields. This should be capable of formation into a ball-field.

"We need only make it up now. We will install it in the 'S Doradus' and the 'Cepheid' as a weapon. We need only install it as an energy source here. Let us start."

CHAPTER TWELVE

Buck Kendall with a slow smile, looked out of the port in the thick metal wall. The magnetic shield of the Lunar Fort was washed constantly with the fires of exploding magnetic bombs. The smile spread broader. "My friends," he said softly, "you can pull from now till doomsday as far as I'm concerned, and you won't even disturb us now." He looked back over his shoulder into the power room. A hunched bulk, beautifully designed and carefully finished, the apparatus that created 'Uncertainty of the Fourth Degree' was destroying matter, and creating by its destruction terrific electric fields. These fields were feeding the magnetic shield now. Under the present drain, the machine was not noticeably working. In fact, Kendall was a bit annoyed. He had tested out the energy generating properties of this machine, trying to find a limit. He had found there was no limit. The great copper conductors, charged with the same atostor force that was used in the mercury fuel, were perfect conductors, they had not heated. But the eleven thousand tons of discharged mercury metal had been completely charged in just a bit better than eleven minutes. The pumps wouldn't force it through the charging apparatus any faster than that.

Two weeks more had passed, while the "S Doradus" and the "Cepheid" were fitted out with the new apparatus Buck had designed. They were almost ready to start now.

McLaurin came down the corridor, and stopped near Kendall. He too smiled at the Miran's attempts. "They've got a long way to go, Buck."

"They're going a long way. Clear back home—and we'll be right along. I don't think they can outdistance us."

"I still don't see why you couldn't use one of those Uncertainty conditions—the First Degree perhaps, and annihilate our inertia."

"You can't control Uncertainty. By its essential character it's beyond control."

"What's that Fourth Degree machine of yours—the material energy—if it isn't controlled and utilized Uncertainty?"

"It's utter and utterly uncontrolled Uncertainty. The matter within that field breaks down to absolutely nothing. Within, no law whatsoever applies, but fortunately, outside the old laws of physics apply—and we can gather and use the energy which is released outside, though nothing can be done inside. Why, think, man, if I could control that Uncertainty, I could do anything at all, absolutely anything. It would be a world as unreasonable as a bad dream. Think how unreasonable those manifestations we first got were!"

"But can't you get any control at all?"

"Very little. Anyway, if I could get inertialess conditions at will, I'd be afraid of them. They'd make chemical reactions impossible in all probability—and life is chemical. Two atoms must come into more or less violent contact before a union takes place, and cannot if they have neither momentum nor inertia.

"Anyway—why worry. I can't do it, because I can't control this thing. And we have the extra-space drive."

"How does that darned thing work? Can't you drop the math and tell me about it?"

Kendall smiled. "Not too readily. Remember first, as to the driving system, that it works on the fabric of space. Space is, in the physical sense, a fabric woven of the threads of lines of force from every body in the universe, made up of fields and forces. It is elastic, and can transmit strains. But anything that can transmit strains, can be strained against. With the tremendous field intensities available by the material engines, I can get such fields as will 'dig their toes' into space and push.

"That's the drive itself. It is accelerationless, because it enfolds us, and acts equally on every atom of us. By maintaining in addition a slight artificial gravity—thanks also to the intensity of those material engine fields—we can be comfortable, while we accelerate at tremendous rates.

"That is, I think, at least allied to the Stranger's system. For the high-speed drive, I do in fact use the Uncertainty. I can control it in a certain sense by determining its powers, and the limits of uncertainty, whether First, Second, Third or Fourth Degree. It advances in jumps— but on a finer plotting of the curve, you can see that each jump represents a vast series of smaller jumps. That is, there is Class A, B, C, D, and so forth Uncertainty of the First Degree. Now Class A First Degree Uncertainty involves only the deepest, broadest principles. Only they break down. One of these is the law of the speed of light.

"I'm sure that isn't the system the Strangers use, but I'm also sure there's no limit to the speed we can get."

"Doesn't that wreck your drive system?"

"No, because gravity and the fields I use in driving are First Degree Uncertainties of the higher classes.

"But at any rate, it will work. And—I suspect you came to say you were ready to go."

"I did." McLaurin nodded.

"Still stick to your original plan?"

McLaurin nodded. "I think it's best. You follow those fellows back to their system in the 'S Doradus' and I'll stay here in the 'Cepheid' to protect the system. They may need some time to get out of the place here. And remember, we ought to be as decent as they were. They didn't bother the transports leaving Jupiter when they came in, only attacked the warships. We're bound to do the same, but we'll have to keep a watch on them, nonetheless. So you go on ahead."

They started down the corridor, and came presently to the huge locks where the "S Doradus" and the "Cepheid" were berthed. The super-ships lay cold and gray now, men swarming in and out with last-minute supplies. Air, water, spare parts, bedding and personal equipment. Douglass, Cole, and most of the laboratory staff would go with Kendall when he followed the Strangers home. Devin and a few of the most advanced physicists would stay with McLaurin in case of need.

An hour later the "S Doradus" rose gently, soundlessly from her berth, and floated out of the open lock-door. The "Cepheid" followed her in five seconds. Still under the great screen of the fort, the lashing, coruscating colors of the magnetic bombs and the magnetic screen flashed and was iridescent. The "S Doradus" poked her great nose gently through the screen, and an instant later her titanically powerful, material-engine effortlessly discharged a great magnetic bomb, sent with the combined power of five atomic-powered interstellar ships. The two ships separated now, the "Cepheid" under McLaurin flashing ahead with sudden, terrific acceleration toward Mars, whispering through space at a speed that made it undetectable, faster than light. The "S Doradus" journeyed out leisurely toward the fleet of forty-seven Miran ships.

Gresth Gkae saw the "S Doradus" and as he watched the steady progress, felt sudden fear at his heart. The ship seemed so certain...

At a distance of thirty thousand miles, Kendall stopped. Magnetic bombs were washing his screen continuously now, seeking to exhaust the ship as all the great ships beyond poured their energy against it. A slow smile spread over Kendall's mouth as he heard the gentle hum of the barely working material-engine. Carefully he aligned the nose UV beam of the "S Doradus" on the nearest of the Miran ships. Then he depressed a switch.

There was no ion-release before the force-mirror now. Just a jet of gas whirling into a half-inch field of "Uncertainty of the Fourth Degree." The matter vanished instantly in released energy so stupendous that the greatest previous UV beams had been harmless things by comparison. Material energy maintained the mirror forces. Material energy gave the power that was released. And only material energy could have stood up before it. Thirty thousand miles away, a Miran ship flamed instantaneously into inconceivable incandescence, vanishing almost in blue-violet light of terrific intensity. The ship reeled away, a half-molten wreck.

The beam spotted two more ships before it winked out. Then Kendall began sending bombs. He moved up to within 2000 miles that his aim might be accurate. They were bombs of "Uncertainty of the Third Degree," the Uncertainty of atomic law in bomb form. One hit the nose of the nearest ship, and a sphere five feet in diameter glowed mistily blue for a moment. Then very easily, the matter that formed the wall of the cruiser began to run and change, and presently there was only a hole, and an expanding cloud of gas. Three more flowed toward it—

and the hole enlarged, and another hole appeared in a bulkhead behind.

Kendall made a change. For the first time there came the staccato bark of the material engine under strain, as it fashioned the terrific fields of "Uncertainty of the Ultimate Degree." Abruptly they leapt out, invisible till they entered a magnetic screen, then run over with opalescent light as the energy of the field was sucked into them and released.

It struck the nose of a ship—a field no larger than an apple...

A titanic gout of energy burst out that was soundless in space. The ship suddenly opened back, opened like the peel of a banana, till a little nub remained at the further end, and the metal flaps dropped back across and behind it dejectedly. A second ship was struck, and it was struck on one side, so that it was shattered like a spent firecracker.

Then the Miran fleet vanished in speed.

Kendall followed them. "I think," he said with a grin, "they tried to use their radio beam, but it spread too much to do anything at that distance. And they used their rotating magnetic field, which we couldn't feel. And their crumbler ray too, of course. I wonder—are they headed only for Jupiter? No—no, they've passed it!"

Faster than light, faster than energy could follow through space, or Uncertainty Bombs pursue, the Mirans were fleeing for home. They knew now that only in speed lay safety. Already they knew that a similar ship had appeared off Jupiter, and, after wiping out the Phobos and Mars stations with one bomb each, had cleared the Jovian Satellites with equal terrible efficiency.

In one of the fleeing ships was a broken, tired old man, and his staff. Gresth Gkae looked back at the blank, distorted space behind them, at the swiftly dwindling sun, and spoke. "I was at fault, my friends. Jarth has spoken. *They* are the stronger and the wiser race. Farth Skalt has shown you—they use space fields of intensity 100. That means the energy of the ultimate destruction. Jarth used us as his instrument of testing, only to drive and stimulate that race. I do not—nay. There is no doubt now, for look."

Plainly visible, rapidly overtaking them, the "S Doradus" appeared sharp, and luminous on the jet of distorted space.

"We cannot escape, my friends. Shall we return to Sthor or remain in space, lost?"

"Let us deflect our course—at least he may not know our destination." The interstellar ship turned very slightly in her course. Plainly they saw the "S Doradus" flash on, in a straight line, headed for distant, red-glowing Mira. Gresth Gkae watched, and shrugged. Silently he put the ship back on its course, at its utmost speed. Parallel with them, near to them, the "S Doradus" flashed on. Day after day, the two hurled through space faster than light. Gradually Mira brightened, and at last became a disc.

Gresth Gkae slowed his ships, and Kendall, watching, slowed to match his speed. Five billion miles from Sthor, they had reached normal space speeds. Viciously the Miran fleet attacked the lone ship from Earth. Their rays, their bombs, their every weapon was flaming. Great interstellar ships flashed suddenly into speeds greater than that of light, seeking to ram and destroy the smaller ship. The "S Doradus" flashed into equal or greater speed, and eluded them.

Kendall had determined now, which was the leader's ship.

Gresth Gkae watched dully as his ships attempted to destroy the single, small ship. He sighed in resignation, and turned to walk back to the chapel aboard the ship. One last prayer to Jarth...

Gresth Gkae stopped abruptly. The great ship was lurching strangely. Men shouted sudden, frightened cries. The clanking and thud of relays sounded, the shrill of alarms. Then the alarms stopped, and suddenly the whole great ship vibrated to an infinitely deep voice speaking in perfect Sthorian. The voice remarked solemnly, in great, vibrant tones, that they would certainly receive news presently from the Expeditions. It went on for some seconds to discuss the conditions as reported in the new system. Then it stopped abruptly. An electric motor just above Gresth Gkae's head suddenly hummed into action without reason or power connection. Almost simultaneously he heard the shouts of startled men as the great lock doors began to open into space of their own accord, bulkhead doors slipped shut as the roar of escaping air echoed in the ship.

Then it was all over. Gresth Gkae ran to the control room. The Mirans there looked up at him with drawn faces.

"The instruments—Gresth Gkae—the instruments. The instruments read impossible things, the motors worked without reason, the fields fluctuated—the atomic engines stopped and the magnetic shield broke down and gripped part of the ship instead!" reported the bewildered pilot.

"I do not know—some strange weapon of—" began the old scientist. Something luminous and huge twisted suddenly through space toward them, a bomb of "Uncertainty of the First Degree." It wrapped the ship silently—and again strange things happened. Abruptly the ship started whirling violently, yet without centrifugal force. The heavens wheeled crazily, and turned about three axes simultaneously. There was no gyroscopic effect to hold them!

Gradually the thing died out. Then a great field seemed to catch the ship, and hurl it away from its companions. Abruptly the pilot applied all his power to pull free. In vain.

Gresth Gkae shook his head slowly, and raised the pilot's hands from the board. "Let them do as they will. I think they mean us no real harm, Thart Kralt. They can, we know, destroy us in an instant. Perhaps he wants us to go somewhere with him…" Gresth Gkae smiled sadly. "…and anyway, we can do nothing."

For nearly a billion miles the great ship was hurled through space at tremendous normal-space velocity. Then abruptly it was halted, without a sign of strain or hurt. The great twenty-foot UV beam on the nose of the "S Doradus" broke into glowing gentle red light. It flashed twice. There was a pause. Then it flashed four times. A long wait. Then three times, a pause and nine times. A wait. Four times, a pause, sixteen times. Then it stopped.

A slow smile of ineffable joy spread over Gresth Gkae's face. "Jarth Be Praised. He can destroy, but does not wish to. Ah, Thart Kralt, turn your spotlight toward him, and flash it twenty-five times, for he is trying to start communications with us. Jarth is wise beyond all understanding. They were the weaker race, and they are the stronger. But also they are the better, for they could destroy, and they do not, but seek only to communicate."

EPILOGUE

The interstellar liner "Mirasol" settled gently to Sthor, having circled wide of Asthor, and from her hold a cargo of the heavy Jovian elements was discharged, while a mixed stream of Solarians and Mirans came from her passenger quarters.

A delegation of Mirans met the new Ambassador from Sol, Commander McLaurin, and conducted him joyfully to the Central Government Group. Beside the great buildings, a battered, scarred interstellar ship lay, her rear section a mass of great patches, rudely applied, and rudely made, mere cast metal plates.

Gresth Gkae welcomed Commander McLaurin to the Government Hall. "Your arrival today, Commander McLaurin, was most fortunate," he said in the interstellar language that had been developed, "for but yesterday Gresth Talak, my brother, arrived in his ship. Before we made that fortunate-unfortunate expedition against your system, we waited for him, and he did not come, so we knew his ship had, like others, been lost.

"He arrived only yesterday, some seventy hours ago, and explained how it had come about. He too found a solar system. But he was less fortunate than I, and while exploring this uninhabited system, far out still from the central sun, where there should have been no masses of matter, one of those rare things, a giant stony meteor that even a magnetic shield will not stop careened into the rear of his ship. Damaged badly, barely able to move, they settled to a planet. The atmosphere was breathable, the temperature mild. But while they could navigate planetary distances, they could not return, so for nearly four and a half of your years they remained there, working, working to repair their ship.

"They have done it at last. And they have returned. And best of all, after a four-year stay there, they know all they need know about that system of eleven planets. It is compact as yours, with an ultra-light sun such as yours, and four of the planets are habitable. Together we can colonize that system! It is a system of stable heat and stable light. And it is small, yet large enough. And with the devices such as your new energy has permitted, we need never fear the stony meteors again." Gresth Gkae smiled happily. "Still better—it is inhabited only by the lowest forms of life. It is too costly to both races when Jarth sees fit to stimulate them by throwing one against the other, despite the good things that may come later."

THE END

If you've enjoyed this book, you will not want to miss these terrific titles...

ARMCHAIR SCI-FI, FANTASY, & HORROR DOUBLE NOVELS, $12.95 each

D-1   **THE GALAXY RAIDERS** by William P. McGivern
           SPACE STATION #1 by Frank Belknap Long

D-2   **THE PROGRAMMED PEOPLE** by Jack Sharkey
           SLAVES OF THE CRYSTAL BRAIN by William Carter Sawtelle

D-3   **YOU'RE ALL ALONE** by Fritz Leiber
           THE LIQUID MAN by Bernard C. Gilford

D-4   **CITADEL OF THE STAR LORDS** by Edmund Hamilton
           VOYAGE TO ETERNITY by Milton Lesser

D-5   **IRON MEN OF VENUS** by Don Wilcox
           THE MAN WITH ABSOLUTE MOTION by Noel Loomis

D-6   **WHO SOWS THE WIND...** by Rog Phillips
           THE PUZZLE PLANET by Robert A. W. Lowndes

D-7   **PLANET OF DREAD** by Murray Leinster
           TWICE UPON A TIME by Charles L. Fontenay

D-8   **THE TERROR OUT OF SPACE** by Dwight V. Swain
           QUEST OF THE GOLDEN APE by Ivar Jorgensen and Adam Chase

D-9   **SECRET OF MARRACOTT DEEP** by Henry Slesar
           PAWN OF THE BLACK FLEET by Mark Clifton.

D-10   **BEYOND THE RINGS OF SATURN** by Robert Moore Williams
           A MAN OBSESSED by Alan E. Nourse

ARMCHAIR SCIENCE FICTION CLASSICS, $12.95 each

C-1   **THE GREEN MAN**
           by Harold M. Sherman

C-2   **A TRACE OF MEMORY**
           By Keith Laumer

C-3   **INTO PLUTONIAN DEPTHS**
           by Stanton A. Coblentz

ARMCHAIR MASTERS OF SCIENCE FICTION SERIES, $16.95 each

M-1   **MASTERS OF SCIENCE FICTION, Vol. One**
           Bryce Walton—"Dark of the Moon" and other tales

M-2   **MASTERS OF SCIENCE FICTION, Vol. Two**
           Jerome Bixby—"One Way Street" and other tales